A MOST DANGEROUS INNOCENCE

FIORELLA DE MARIA

A Most Dangerous Innocence

A Novel

IGNATIUS PRESS   SAN FRANCISCO

Cover photograph:
Woolwich Polytechnic Gymnasium, 1911
© Bridgeman Images

Cover design by John Herreid

© 2019 Ignatius Press, San Francisco
ISBN 978-1-62164-257-2
Library of Congress Control Number 2018949813
Printed in the United States of America ∞

I

The girl stared out of the grimy train window, too absorbed by the sight of the disappearing London platform to turn her head and acknowledge the newcomer into the carriage. Harry Forbes, for his part, could hardly hide his disappointment at the presence of a fellow traveller, but he had caught his train at the last possible moment as always, and by the time he had deposited his trunk with a porter and staggered along the narrow corridor in search of a seat, there had been no other empty compartments. Somehow it did not feel quite right to sit alone in the company of a schoolgirl, but it would be rude to heave the door back open and retreat now that she had heard him come in. He sat down awkwardly on the opposite seat, as close to the door as humanly possible.

The girl had a thick, unruly bob of black curls she had not bothered to pin away from her face, and he noticed that she seemed in the habit of constantly shaking her head from side to side to keep it out of her eyes. Her straw hat had been carelessly tossed aside and sat next to her gas mask and a small knapsack. Harry's discomfort grew as he noted the blue-and-white stripes on the hatband and the school crest —a shield with a dolphin and three stars. She was a Mulwith girl then, and possibly soon to be one of his pupils. They faced a lengthy journey in one another's company, and he suspected he ought to attempt some conversation with her, but she made no effort to turn her fixed stare from the window, where houses and chimneys were hurtling over the horizon.

Harry busied himself lifting his own gas mask and leather holdall into the overhead rack. He hoped the girl was not the type to be overcome by homesickness on a journey to school; he was young enough to remember those childhood battles with tears, the counting of hours and minutes until the miserable time of departure. The girl was old enough to have adapted to the perpetual meetings and partings of boarding school life by now, but girls could be quite unpredictable about such things, and he had an irrational fear of being alone with a sobbing female, uncertain as to whether he should tell her to pull herself together or make some effort to console her.

Harry had just removed his coat and begun folding it carefully, placing it beside him under his hat, when the dark head turned slowly to look at him. "Good afternoon," she said in a clear voice, regarding him intently with dry, calm eyes. "I wonder if you might put my bag up there too, if it's not too much trouble?"

"Certainly, young lady," he answered, taking a step back. It was a perfectly reasonable request for her to make, since he was a good deal taller and stronger than she, but he felt unnerved at the thought that he was taking orders from a pupil. She was at a troubling stage, he thought, but he gave her a friendly smile and gathered up her belongings regardless, leaving the hat where it was in case it might be damaged in the luggage rack. He could not quite place her age; he suspected she might be nearing the end of her schooldays, but her uniform marked out the divide between them, and Harry could not quite work out whether she had had any business setting him a task to perform for her.

"Thank you, sir," she answered, with reassuring deference, as he sat back down with a pencil and the *Times* crossword. "I'm afraid I find those racks a little difficult to reach." With that, she picked up a book, closing the conversation as abruptly as she had started it.

"Not at all," said Harry to her lowered head. He shifted his position carefully so that he could get a better look at her whilst appearing to be glancing at his paper. She was a girl who clearly enjoyed good health; her complexion was bright and ruddy from hours spent outside, but there was something about her colouring that suggested a foreign influence. He might have thought her of Celtic origin on account of the black curls, but her eyes were ebony black rather than blue, and her skin tones were tawny like a Renaissance Madonna. His gaze was drawn to a discreet gold necklace, the pendant—a six-pointed star—visible against the starched collar of her tunic. "That's an interesting necklace," he said, his curiosity strong enough to overcome his earlier reserve. "Very pretty."

"It was a birthday present from my father," she explained, lowering her book. She seemed to remember her manners all of a sudden and extended a hand to him. "Forgive me. I'm Judith Randall. How d'you do?"

He shook her hand. "How do you do, Judith? I'm Mr Forbes. I'm on my way to Mulwith School too."

"Everyone calls me Judy," Judy responded, looking at him in faint recognition. "You're the new mathematics master, replacing Miss Taylor. I'm rather afraid I've lost my bet."

"Bet?"

"Yes. I bet Beryl Craven an aniseed ball that you'd be old. When Miss Miller said she'd had to employ a second chap to the staff on account of all things being rationed—schoolmistresses included—you would have to be old like Mr Peterson. How old are you?"

"That's rather impertinent, don't you think?" answered Harry, determined to introduce some control over the situation. "And Mr Peterson is hardly old, as I recall from our brief meeting. Barely a day over fifty."

"Exactly. Old." She hesitated, a little reticent after the reprimand. "He doesn't really count, anyhow. He is only a Mulwith teacher because Mrs Peterson is the games' mistress—she's terrific, by the way—and he has to live there of course. So, he might as well teach whilst he's on the property. He speaks hundreds of languages." She gave him a suspicious glance. "Oughtn't you to be a soldier?"

"Now that really is overstepping the mark," said Harry, picking up his newspaper again. She shrugged her shoulders with a look that said "please yourself", then stared a little sulkily out of the window. "I shall have to keep an eye on you by the look of things. I shan't have any insolence in my classroom."

"You shan't have any trouble from me," she promised without a hint of conciliation in her voice. "I won the mathematics cup last term. I'm good at numbers."

Harry chuckled, thinking how many times he had heard a boast like that in his short teaching career. "Really? What's thirty-four plus one hundred and forty-five?"

"One hundred and seventy-nine. Easy."

"Four hundred and twenty-six plus five hundred and eighty-seven?"

She didn't miss a beat. "One thousand and thirteen."

"Seven thousand three hundred and twenty plus two hundred and fifty-nine?"

"Seven thousand five hundred and seventy-nine. I say, do you mind?"

"Sorry." He watched as she glanced back at the window, aware that he had overdone things. "Is there anything I should know about the school?"

But Judy had clearly lost interest in the conversation and did not look back at him. "I hope you've brought food with you; you'll be hungry," she ventured. "And you'd best stay out of Miss Miller's way. She's evil."

Harry forced a laugh. "I'll bear that in mind." He waited for her to speak again, but she was absorbed in her own thoughts, and he thought it better to leave her in peace.

~

Judy stared out at the rolling hills, awaiting the sudden sight of the sea in the distance where the track traversed the brow of the Gog Magog Hills and wound itself along the coast. She loved the countryside, but on the journey to school those lovely hills and trees were merely signposts pointing ever farther away from London and home. Even the sight of the sea, when it came, offered little cheer. She could just make out the trails of barbed wire that were slowly snaking their way along England's coastline, and she lost count of the number of squat, ugly pillboxes they had passed.

Judy had never liked boarding school, but so few children of any age truly enjoyed that wrench from family and the freedom of the holidays. It was hard for her to see what there was to enjoy about the brutal exchange of home's happy

9

cosiness for the spartan world of lousy food and rigid timetables marked out by the ringing of bells and the barking of
commands. But she had never been the sort of child who
blubbed for her mother or spent the early days of the term
tormented by homesickness. Home was pleasant enough,
but more for the creature comforts it offered than any sen-
timental reasons. Since her mother's death five years before,
Judy's father had busied himself in war work, those endless
secret preparations for the inevitable, all being worked out
whilst the rest of the populace had celebrated Peace for Our
Time. In the absence of adult supervision, Judy had come to
enjoy having the run of the city, staying at friends' houses,
living by her own rules and timetables. The return to school
was always going to be an unwelcome breach with life as
she believed it ought to be led.

But now Britain was at war, though she could have been
forgiven for failing to notice during those early uneasy
months after the declaration: *We are at war with Germany . . .*
Judy had had the sinking feeling when her father had seen
her off at the station at the start of the new academic year,
then again after Christmas and even more so now, that she
was being got out of the way.

"I feel like one of those evacuees!" she had protested to
her father during one of their rare walks together. They had
passed a gaggle of chattering little boys in their school caps,
armed with cases and paper bags containing a meagre lunch.
They might have been little ones on their way to school but
for the labels around their necks.

"You're nothing of the sort!" answered her father, giving
her a dismissive wave of the hand. "You're always making
mountains out of molehills. You're going to school as you

have done at the start of every term since you were seven years old. It's the same as it has always been."

"I'm sixteen; I want to help with the war effort. If you gave permission . . ."

"No, no, not this nonsense again. What on earth do you imagine a thing like you could do anyway?"

"I'm sorry; I forgot," she sneered back, capturing his tone perfectly. She turned her back on him, taking a few noisy steps in the opposite direction, but it did not occur to her how childish she was being. "I'm a *thing*, aren't I? I'm only a child!"

It never took long for David Randall to lose patience in a disagreement with his daughter, mostly because he felt affronted by the idea of her questioning him at all. However, he had been quicker than usual to start belittling her and felt an unwelcome surge of temper at the sight of her turned back. David was a tall, wiry individual, and he covered the ground between them in two easy strides, grabbing her wrist to force her to turn around. "If we weren't in a public place, I'd give you precisely the answer you deserve," he hissed. He caught sight of the little gold star she had requested for her birthday, which had the effect of sending his anger over an invisible tipping point. "And I don't know what you wanted with that ridiculous trinket either! You're not a Jewess. One Jewish grandmother doesn't count, and even *she* was baptised."

Judy gazed up at him with an all-too-familiar look of reproach. "In Germany it counts, doesn't it? Oh, please do let go!"

David looked down at his own hand, which was still wrapped tightly around his daughter's wrist. He immediately loosened his grip, cursing himself for hurting her. "Forgive me. I didn't mean it."

Judy let her hands drop to her sides and continued walking, signalling to him that the matter was closed. "We should get home. I'm awfully hungry."

David was not a man to whom affectionate feelings came easily, but he felt a quiet sense of despair watching his daughter out of the corner of his eye, walking in step with him just a few feet away. She was still a child, even if she did not feel like it, but it would not be long at all before she was gone to who knew what fate with the world in the state it was in. He had tried to hide the reports of the persecution of the Jews in Germany and elsewhere, but she had a tendency to find things out and had characteristically taken it all to heart. "If the Jews in Poland have to wear a star, let me wear one."

"How can you possibly know that?"

"Dr Radish told me."

"It's Dr Rakowicz! You can't even say his name properly!"

"No offence, everyone calls him that."

Another argument, another battleground that had opened up between them. She was giving herself an identity based upon the lunatic views of the National Socialists, but as usual she had the bit between her teeth and would not let the matter pass. Yes, she said, she was a Catholic, but she was also a Jew, and the Blessed Virgin was a Jewess. She had fled the room before he could command her to get out of his sight, which perhaps had been fortunate. And then he had felt guilty for losing his temper and had bought her the wretched star after all.

Their parting at the station had unsettled Judy. She was used to her father giving her a formal send-off at the beginning of term, getting her to the station, seeing her safely onto the train and perhaps patting her arm or giving her a perfunctory hug before he walked away. On this occasion, she had sensed for the first time that he was reluctant to let her go. He had hovered at the door of her carriage, holding her hand as they waited for the whistle to blow, an odd-enough gesture for him at the best of times. "I'm sorry, Judy," he had said sadly. "I'm so sorry if I've been harsh with you. I'm afraid it's a bad time to be a father."

She had felt embarrassed and tried to cut him off. "Oh, don't worry, Daddy, there's nothing to—"

"I only want you to be safe, you see," he continued, as though she had not spoken. "If the Germans take England, it will be very terrible, especially for women, especially for the Jews. I might not be there to protect you when it comes to it."

Judy listened for the sound of the whistle, but no such reprieve came. "It'll be all right, Daddy. Please don't say these things."

"I know you don't like school, but you're safe there. I want you to be well away from all of this."

"I should find a seat," she said lamely, desperate for him to go, but when she had settled herself in the last empty compartment, she was unnerved to see that he was still standing on the platform, watching her through the window.

The war was making everyone behave strangely, Judy reassured herself, fingering the star around her neck. She would not be allowed to wear it with her uniform once she got to school, but the chain was long enough that she thought she might be able to tuck it under her clothes so that no one would know about it. That somewhat defeated the point of the thing, of course—she wanted it to be seen, but she would have to think very hard before provoking Miss Miller's wrath again in a hurry.

Judy was still smarting from the consequences of the food strike she had masterminded during the previous term, though she liked to think that her actions had improved the sewage they were served on china plates every dinnertime. It had taken some courage for the members of her table to stand in silence, refusing to sit down after grace and tuck in. Every scrap of food on every plate at the table had to be eaten before the girls could be excused, so a refusal even to start the meal was an act of defiance beyond anything the girls had ever tried before.

Strange how Miss Miller had known it was her, pondered Judy. When Matron had asked them sharply what they thought they were doing, it had been Beatrice who had answered her question; yet when Matron had gone to summon Miss Miller, the old trout had not even stopped to question the girls about whose bright idea it had been in the first place. Miss Miller had stalked straight into the room amid the hushed panic of the entire refectory and scanned their stony faces for a second or two before grabbing Judy by a fistful of her obliging hair and frog-marching her in the direction of her study. *How could she have known?* She had never attempted such a stunt before; but the fact was that Miss Miller had been absolutely correct, and Judy could hardly complain about being assigned menial tasks and being forced to eat apart from the others. Miss Miller had, however, made it abundantly clear that she would like nothing better than an excuse to throw her out of her splendid school, and Judy had better watch her step.

The train was snaking its way along the coast now, allowing Judy to look directly out to sea without having to witness the pollution of the beaches by concertina wire or whatever it was called. "The war is just across the sea," she said aloud, then blushed, remembering that she had company.

Harry Forbes looked up with a start, having also blanked out the existence of the other occupant. "Well—yes, yes it is. Not quite in that direction of course, but yes, across the Channel."

"It's not far at all."

"Far enough, thank God. Let's just be grateful it hasn't come to us yet."

"That's a dreadful thing to say!" she burst out, startling him. "Think of all those people dying over there! It's all right for you—you're not fighting!"

Harry threw down his paper in a manner that was intended to intimidate her, but she did not flinch. He had a nasty feeling that she was the sort of girl who had no respect for men whatsoever, having grown up in an exclusively female environment that saw the male of the population as irrelevant and pretty revolting. She had, however, hit a nerve, and she was clearly too bright for it to have been accidental. "You're a little young to be so indignant about matters that are none of your business, don't you think?"

He waited for her to shrink back or apologise, but she glanced impassively at him before turning her attention to his discarded paper. She had the cheek to pick it up and appear to start reading it. "Are you stuck on those clues?" she asked as though the previous exchange had not happened.

He snatched it back. "I'm sure I'll manage, thank you."

"Endymion."

"I beg your pardon?"

"Clue: 'Finish day at last, composer becomes shepherd.' The answer is 'Endymion'. I had to write out the whole blasted poem as a punishment once."

Harry picked up his pencil and wrote the word in the space provided, irritated to discover that it fitted perfectly. "Very clever," he answered with poor grace he immediately regretted. "All right, how about 'Stay put to see one race in view'."

"Word length?"

"Two words, three and five. Second letter of the first word will be *I*."

She closed her eyes for dramatic effect. " 'Sit tight'. The double *T* refers to the Isle of Man race."

" 'Prune condiment to meet expectations'. Word len—"

" 'Cut the mustard'," Judy put in. She decided not to tell her new teacher that she had completed the crossword earlier that morning with her father at the breakfast table. She had indeed had to copy out that poem and knew it painfully well, but she would never have worked out the reference to the motorcycling race.

Harry filled the final empty white boxes in awed silence. He would have liked to have believed it was her way of making amends, but he suspected she was giving him a very different message indeed. All in all, Harry was beginning to wish he had taken an earlier train. "Are all the girls at Mulwith like you?" he asked testily. He could suddenly see himself in front of a class of pert young girls with the same soulful eyes, deep enough to hold the universe, and razor-sharp minds ready to cut him down to size every time he made a mistake.

"Oh no," she assured him, "I'm the school madcap. This is our station, by the way."

Thank God for that, he thought, taking the girl's things down from the rack before snatching up his own and making his way out into the corridor. *One madcap I can tolerate; a school full of them, and I'd sooner face the bloody Germans.*

Judy watched in horror as her new maths master walked away, and felt herself blushing with shame. The limp was not at all pronounced, and he had evidently learnt to conceal the stiffness in his left foot, but the telltale signs of childhood polio were obvious. She had given him good cause to make her life a misery for the rest of the term, she thought, and part of her almost hoped he would.

2

The first morning of the term dawned bright and cold. The early morning was the only time the dormitory looked almost homey, the way the pale sunlight filtered through the high windows making long slanted patterns across the room. There were thirty beds in Judy's dorm, ten along both the long sides and five at either end, with the end beds being the least popular on account of offering very little privacy to the occupant. Each steel-framed bed with its horsehair mattress and starched white bedsheets was accompanied by a small bedside cabinet in which the girls could store their few personal effects, and a sign showing the girl's name and serial number. The white walls bore no decorations or pictures, giving the impression of a hospital ward, an illusion helped greatly by Matron's ample presence, walking among the rows of sleeping bodies in her spotless blue-and-white uniform, every trace of hair scraped under a white bonnet.

Judy, up with the lark as ever, was already gingerly getting herself into her gymslip when Matron approached her bed, having intended to wake her. Matron, a kindly woman widowed during the Great War, had spent years channelling her maternal warmth into caring for other people's daughters, and Judy felt an instinctive affection towards her in spite of her obsessive enforcement of every possible rule and regulation. "Is your watch right?" whispered Matron. "Make sure you keep a close eye on the time."

"Yes, Matron, I will."

"And don't wander. Remember what happened last time."

Judy stifled a giggle. The conclusion to that early morning dalliance had been eye watering, as she recalled, but she was always amused by Matron's concern to keep her out of Miss Miller's way. "I'll keep to the grounds. I promise."

Judy sat back on her bed and slipped on her stockings and running shoes. Nearby, her friend Beatrice stirred but quickly returned to her slumbers. None of the girls would be easy to wake when the reveille bell rang that morning— they were tired by their respective journeys and the struggle to return to timetable again—but Judy tiptoed out into the middle of the dorm as carefully as she could, avoiding the floorboards she knew creaked. Matron was at her elbow again, brandishing an ominously uncorked bottle and spoon. "Oh please, Matron, is this really necessary?" whispered Judy. She could smell the cod-liver oil and malt already, and her stomach churned. "It makes me frightfully queasy."

Matron did not deign to answer, handed her the spoon and began pouring out the thick dark liquid. "Come on now, you're a big girl. Take it!"

∽

She was a big girl, Judy thought bitterly, as she fled the building and ran down the beech-lined avenue towards the outer perimeter of the school grounds. She was a big girl with Matron doling out ghastly medicine that tasted as though it belonged inside the engine of a transatlantic liner. She was a big girl indeed! But it was difficult to brood even on the first day of term with eleven miserable weeks stretching out like a Dante-esque Purgatory. The sky was gloriously clear, promising a perfect May morning, and Judy could hear the twitter of birds in the trees as she got into a rhythm and lengthened her strides as far as she could manage. She knew she was out of sight of the school building by now and jumped off the stony path onto the forbidden territory of the grass—jumping down was the simplest way to avoid the risk of slipping—swerving around a patch of glowing marigolds as she made her way down the short slope that took her onto the bridleway.

The bridleway marked the outer edge of the school grounds. There was no fence, but it was a long-established school rule that no girl was to cross the bridleway into the combe. There was a good reason for this, though Judy did not know it then: a girl from the school had been attacked many years before when she had wandered into the combe and darkness had fallen, causing her to lose her way, but the girls were kept innocent of the knowledge. Judy glanced at her watch to calculate whether she could risk going out-of-bounds, jogging on the spot as she made the decision. She was loath to break her promise to Matron only because she knew Matron hated to see the girls in trouble and Miss Miller would relish an opportunity to hold her back after assembly. But the combe was so lovely at this time of year—she could smell the moist soil and the fresh leaves still damp with dew, all those overpowering aromas of a late spring morning she had almost forgotten about in London. It was still very early; she had at least half an hour before she needed to be back in the dorm to change and prepare for breakfast. She skipped across the bridleway in three little jumps and disappeared between the hedgerows under the dank cover of the trees.

It was sports day in just five days' time, held early in the term to celebrate the return to school but giving just enough time to practice, though few girls took athletics quite as seriously as Judy. As a child, she had longed to be able to fly, imagining the freedom it might be possible to attain with a pair of downy wings attached to one's shoulders. She had spent many hours lost in her own head, imagining herself soaring into the firmament like Icarus (but never too close to the sun), watching the sights of majestic London slipping by beneath her feet with the long, ambling line of the Thames pulling her along like the ribbon of her own life.

Now that she had left her childhood behind and her fertile imagination with it, Judy found that running was the closest she could come to the freedom of flying, and it had become her passion. It had not been hard to gain permission to run before breakfast, as the school was keen that the girls keep themselves fit, especially in these troubled times, but she knew she might lose the privilege if she were late without good reason. She glanced at her watch from time to time to check when it was time to turn back.

She cleared the dense green tunnel and crossed a blue carpet of speedwells, knocking off hundreds of tiny flower heads as she ran, before turning down a winding lane that opened out onto the coastal path. She had ten minutes before she had to turn back, or she would not have enough time. Ten minutes to run out in the bracing sea air along the craggy shelf that overhung the now-inaccessible beach. She allowed herself to stop for the first time to enjoy the view of the sea shimmering in the morning light, drinking in long salty breaths as she did so.

Judy heard the crackle of twigs underfoot behind her a

second before a gloved hand covered her mouth, stifling her surprised shriek. It was immediately apparent that the assailant meant her no harm; she was able to push the man's hand away from her face and turn around to look at him without meeting any resistance. A white-haired man in an aged military uniform Judy did not recognise stood over her looking almost as surprised as she. He was accompanied by two others of a similar age, also wearing military-style clothes; she glanced instinctively at their hands and noticed that the two men were armed with a rifle and a pistol that must have dated from the previous war, whereas the man who had apprehended her carried a knife that might have seen service against the Zulus.

"What are you playing at, jumping on me like that?" she demanded, finding her voice with some difficulty. "You scared me half to death!"

"You don't look nearly scared enough," said the man with the knife. "Perhaps you knew we were coming."

Judy felt a little dizzy, which she would ordinarily have put down to exercising on an empty stomach, but her mind swam with confusion. The man was obviously English, speaking with a local accent, and his officious manner made her think immediately that she must be in the wrong somehow. Perhaps this was Miss Miller's latest ingenious idea to keep her charges in line, employing retired soldiers to police the boundaries of the school. Then again, they could just be robbers. "I haven't any money, if that's what you're after. We're not allowed to carry any."

"We're not common criminals, missy!" the man with the knife responded, sounding quite offended, but his companion—a small man with thick spectacles—was touching his arm. "Put the knife away, Jack," he said gently. "She's only a kiddie. You're frightening her."

It had not occurred to Judy how terrified she must look, but she immediately became aware that she was not standing up straight and was hugging her arms in front of her. "I'm not afraid of you!" she snapped, confirming their suspicions. "But I should like to know who you are and what you think you're doing!"

"We're defending the realm, my dear," said Jack, making an elaborate show of sheathing his knife. "Now, we're not going to hurt you, but . . . what the devil are you laughing at?"

It was almost certainly nerves and a touch of light-headedness, but Judy was overcome by a fit of the giggles. "God help us if that's true!" she managed to splutter, stepping back towards the path that led to the school. The only remaining fear she had was that this conversation was going to make her late. "Now, if you'll excuse me, gentlemen, I have to get back to school."

Judy turned on her heel and was about to start running again when the same gloved hand came down on her shoulder. "Just a minute, my girl. We haven't finished yet!"

"Oh, please let me go!" she protested. "I shall be late for breakfast!"

"This won't take a minute. Just hand over your papers."

Judy wriggled free. "Why?"

"Nothing personal, but you might be a German spy."

"*What?* Do I look like a German spy to you?"

"They come in all shapes and sizes, you know, and you're obviously not English."

There were few more offensive statements the old man

could have made; Judy's temper flared at the unintended insult. "I've had enough of this. Oh, for goodness' sake, will you—"

"Just hand over your identity card, and we'll let you go," said Jack, physically dragging her away from the path. "There's no use struggling like that, we've a right to ask."

"I don't have my card with me. My gymslip has no pockets! Will you let go!"

"You know it's against the law to go out without it."

Judy attempted to throw the man off, but he showed remarkable strength for a person of such great age, and he forced her arms behind her back. "You're not real soldiers!" she shouted, resisting the urge to drop to her knees to ease the pressure on her shoulders. She could hear approaching footsteps and prayed the right person would walk towards them. Someone was coming, someone was going to intervene to stop this madness. She could only hope it would be a teacher who was likely to be on her side.

"What are you doing with that girl?" roared a male voice. *Thank you, guardian angel*, thought Judy, as the man holding her let go, so abruptly that she fell flat on her face. It was Mr Peterson, the languages master and one of her few allies; she heard the footfalls of Chester, his faithful Labrador, trotting towards her, a moment before a black furry head nuzzled up against her face. "What do you think you're doing?"

"We were only doing our duty. She doesn't have her papers on her," bleated Jack, but when Judy looked round, the three men looked palpably embarrassed; she had no idea where the two guns had gone.

Mr Peterson stooped forward and extended a hand to her. "On your feet, girl. It's all right." She scrambled to her feet and immediately dashed to his side. "You can clearly see she's a Mulwith girl. I'm prepared to vouch that there are no Jerry spies in my school."

"I'm sorry, guv, but she wouldn't hand over her identity card."

"You have no authority to ask for it," answered Mr Peterson sternly. He was using the tone he reserved for miscreants at the back of the class when they refused to pay attention. "I understand that you wish to do your duty, and I commend you for it, but this was needlessly heavy-handed."

"This is not Mulwith land," said Jack. "If she wanders off school property . . ."

"She *has* wandered out-of-bounds, but that is a school matter, and I will deal with her myself. Under no circumstances will you touch any of my pupils again. Is that understood?"

Judy felt her teacher taking her firmly by the elbow, propelling her back in the direction of the school. She had been grateful not to be on the receiving end of that particular dressing down but had a nasty feeling that worse was coming her way. "I'm awfully sorry, sir," she put in, when they were out of earshot.

"I sincerely hope you are, you silly girl!" remarked Mr Peterson. "You know perfectly well where the boundaries of this school are. How long have you been a pupil here?"

"I'm so sorry, sir. It was just such a beautiful morning; I felt as though the sun were calling me—"

"Oh, don't talk such rubbish!" he cut in. "You were never much of a poet. It was disobedience pure and simple. You are granted permission to go out running on the understanding that you can be trusted to keep the rules. Do you understand?"

"Yes, sir." Judy glanced at her watch. "Oh no, I'm late. She'll have my guts for garters"

"Well, that's your own silly fault, isn't it? What are you going to do—skip breakfast and hope Miss Miller fails to notice, or creep in late and hope she is not there when you do so?"

Judy's bedraggled hopes soared. "You're not going to tell her, then?"

Mr Peterson groaned. "I have no particular desire to see you in trouble on your first day back, but if she asks, you know I'll tell her."

"Thanks."

"No need to sound so resentful. You chose to break the rules; you can be a big girl and take the consequences."

"Miss Miller hates me!" Judy whined. The school was coming into view and reminded her unhelpfully of Castle Dracula for a moment.

"Don't be so ridiculous. Why would she?" Mr Peterson came to a halt at the garden gate of the cottage he shared with his wife and children. "Here's where I leave you. Good luck sneaking in."

"Thanks," said Judy miserably. "Much obliged."

"Cheer up—it might never happen! By the way, Annie asked if you wanted to come for tea on Saturday after prep."

Judy immediately felt a little better. Tea with the Petersons was generous enough to see her through much of the following week, and Annie, the Petersons' youngest, had been a firm friend and fellow conspirator for years. "Oh yes, please, I should like that very much. Thank you, sir."

"On your way now."

Judy dashed to the door nearest her dormitory as quick as a flash and crept in as quietly as could be. There was no sound from the dormitory, and when she consulted her watch she knew that the entire school would be tucking into breakfast without her, and there was probably no point in her attempting to sneak in now. She would have to go hungry until lunchtime and hope no one would hear her stomach rumbling during morning maths. She cleared the main corridor—the most dangerous part of the journey—and turned into the narrow passage that led past the bathrooms to the dormitory at the end . . . directly into Miss Miller's waiting arms.

~

Judy's hands always started throbbing the moment she stepped through the door to Miss Miller's study. She saw it as nature's way of forcing her to anticipate the worst-case scenario before it inevitably happened. It was a pity because it should have been quite a pleasant room; it was richly decorated with a mahogany desk, several heaving bookcases and a small metal safe built into the wall, leaving an immense space, large enough for the entire staff to congregate for meetings. For that purpose, there were chairs in a row against the long sides of the room, but Judy did not attempt to sit down, as she knew she would not be invited to do so.

"Well, you've certainly excelled yourself," declared Miss Miller, seating herself at her desk. "You have been back at school a full fifteen hours before finding yourself here. What do you have to say for yourself?" She looked quizzically at Judy. "What are you doing?"

Judy had already held out her hands, palms upwards. "I thought I'd save time."

"Put them away, you cretin, and listen to me."

Judy let her hands swing to her sides. She regarded Miss Miller carefully as she inked her pen and began writing an indecipherable note, searching for clues about what was coming. For a woman who put the fear of God in everyone she encountered—teachers as well as pupils, Judy suspected —Miss Miller was a remarkably birdlike person to look at, with a thin, sunken face made all the narrower by the eccentric hairstyle she had adopted years ago: thin, dark grey hair pinned into a tight bun with a wispy fringe that hung low across her forehead. Rumour had it that the fringe concealed smallpox scars, but even Judy, who had faced her on many occasions over the years, had never got a close-enough look to find out. "Are you giving me lines?" she asked, to Miss Miller's bowed head. Judy's worst horror was lines, worse than any other horrible penance any authority figure could possibly think up for her. She was of such an impatient disposition that nothing distressed her more than sitting at a desk for hours, writing some meaningless command over and over hundreds of times—the tedious waste of time, all that beautiful, precious time frittered away. Unfortunately, Miss Miller had worked out where Judy's weak spots were years ago and was fond of handing that particular task to her.

"No lines today, you'll be relieved to hear," answered Miss Miller without looking up. "It is sports day coming up, as you can hardly have failed to notice."

Judy felt her heart turning somersaults. "Oh, please don't stop me from taking part! I'm sorry I wandered off this morning. I meant to get back in good time, but there—"

"You will of course take part," she continued, as though she had not heard Judy's protestations. "It is most important

29

that you do take part. On the morning of the event, I will give you a small, painless task to perform, and you may then consider the whole matter closed."

"A small task?" echoed Judy, but her head was swimming again. There was never anything remotely painless about any instruction Miss Miller gave. She knew there had to be a catch somewhere, but she had hardly been given much of an idea of what would be expected. "What sort of task?"

"Nothing to be afraid of, but it is very important. You will do precisely as I ask you, to the letter. It won't hurt, and it will not take up any of your precious time, but it is important that you obey it."

"Can't you tell me what it is?" pressed Judy as firmly as she dared. "It might help if I could prepare . . ."

"There's no need," answered Miss Miller, dismissively. "It will take no effort whatsoever on your part, and it may be best if you do not have time to prepare."

Now Judy was desperate to get to the truth of the matter. "What if I can't do it?"

Miss Miller looked up at her, narrowing her eyes. "Oh, you'll do it. You will not have any trouble with that. But if you don't, you will wish you had not returned to school at all. Now, get out or you'll be late for class."

Judy did not have the nerve to linger, and fled the room, half-wondering whether it would not have been easier to beg for lines and have done with it. Miss Miller's request could only spell trouble for Judy, but for the life of her she could not imagine what the old hag was planning.

3

Judy's sense of impending doom did not lift over the weekend, in spite of an enjoyable afternoon with the Peterson family. It had not helped that Mrs Peterson had no idea what Miss Miller was talking about and looked quite rattled by the news when Judy talked to her about it over the washing up.

Mrs Peterson was the sort of unflappable female one expected to find in charge of sport, and she had gained Judy's immediate respect during her first summer term, when another girl had succeeded in putting a javelin through her own foot. Mrs Peterson had dealt adeptly with the injured party, the copious amounts of blood and twenty screaming girls, preventing anyone from fainting with the terse remark: "And if any of you even *thinks* of having a fit of the vapours, you'll run ten laps around the track." She was the tallest woman Judy had ever met, at slightly under the great six-foot mark, and it was a school joke that she had married Mr Peterson only because he was the only man she could find who was tall enough to allow her to wear heels— not that she ever did. She only ever raised her voice to call across a netball court or a playing field, and when she did, it had the clear, commanding air of a respected officer who can expect immediate obedience. All in all, tall, coolheaded Mrs Peterson was an easy person to trust with disturbing information.

"Are you absolutely sure that was what she said?" she had asked, passing Judy a dessert plate to dry. "She's not mentioned any little tasks to me."

"I'm absolutely sure. She said it was a little task that wouldn't be painful or difficult, but if I didn't do it I'd regret ever returning to school."

Annie was at Judy's side, acting as the final part of the human washing-up chain. Mother was washing, Judy was drying and Annie was putting away. Mr Peterson, of course, was performing the vital task of sitting in another room reading the newspaper. "I think she's up to something," declared Annie, flouncing over to the cupboard. "She's never liked Judy."

"Come now, I don't think we need to start imagining any little conspiracies," said Mrs Peterson, who privately could not stand Miss Miller but felt under a professional obligation to hide her feelings. "I daresay she just wants you to help out in some way."

"But why not say so?" Annie put in. She was a charming, lanky girl who always seemed to take up far more space than was strictly necessary. The two girls had been painted by nature from opposite sides of the palette—Annie tall like her parents, with silver-blonde hair that hung in millions of obedient straight lines about her head, Judy the small dark creature who in a film would no doubt be the naughty little sister—but they rarely left one another's side, and Judy's only regret was that Annie always had to disappear home at the end of the day. "If it was something harmless, why not just tell her so?"

Mrs Peterson shrugged. "Well, don't let it unsettle you. I want you on top form on sports day."

32

It was easy enough for Mrs Peterson to say that, thought Judy, checking her laces for the umpteenth time before heading over to the field. She wasn't the one bracing herself for a message from Miss Miller that was sure to ruin the day. Judy tilted her head back to let the warm sunshine touch her face, desperate to recover some of her usual sports day excitement. The weather was perfect; the refreshments tent gleamed promisingly near the sports pavilion, though she suspected the food and drink on offer would be rather drearier than in previous years. Standing in a noisy group at the far end of the track, her house team was gathering, waiting for her.

"There you are, Judy!" called Angela, the house captain, giving her an impatient wave. "First race is in five minutes. I hope you've warmed up!"

"Naturally," promised Judy, enjoying the fleeting pleasure of feeling wanted. The girls of the school belonged to one of four houses and were permitted to field two competitors per form for each event. Judy was down to run in several races on behalf of her house, but the first was her signature race—the four hundred yards—and she would be running it alongside Annie, who with longer legs but poorer stamina and technique would come a close second. It was sure to give Nightingale House a good first score to start the day.

"Best take your marks, girls," said Angela. "Good luck. We'll be cheering you on!"

Judy and Annie hurried over to the start, where the competitors for the other houses were limbering up. Judy noticed that Mr Forbes was approaching slowly, armed with the starting pistol, perhaps because it might be bad form for Mrs Peterson to supervise her own daughter's race. Out of the corner of her eye, Judy could see Miss Miller approaching her from the opposite side and felt a pulse racing in her neck. She tried to pretend she could not see her, willing Mr Forbes to call them to their marks before she arrived, but he had seen her too and was going to wait until she had cleared the area before starting the race.

A hand tapped Judy on the arm, forcing her to turn to the side. "Come second," whispered Miss Miller in her ear. "Run a good race and come second. Annie is going to win."

Judy let out a gasp, but Miss Miller had already walked clear of the track and was taking her place under the shelter of an elm tree. "On your marks!" called Mr Forbes. There was no time to protest or think over what she had been told. Judy braced herself to run, squeezing her fists together to stop her limbs shaking. "Get set!" She took a split-second, sidelong glance at Annie, wondering if Annie was aware of the whole thing; then the starting pistol gave its familiar crack, and she hurtled along the track.

Instinct took over all at once. She saw the blur of her housemates in their sunny yellow colours cheering uproariously as she dashed past them; she felt the thunder of her heart almost matching the rhythm of her feet as she ran, the delicious sensation of her blood pounding through her veins like some primordial battle hymn to life. At the first corner, Judy broke ahead of the other runners, in line with her usual strategy. By the time she had run the first long stretch of track, there was no longer any other runner within her field of vision. As she turned, she judged that there was well over a yard between herself and the close line of the other athletes.

Whatever reason Miss Miller could possibly have for forcing her to lose, it was lost in the overwhelming instinct of the runner to cross that finishing line. Judy ran and ran as though the devil were at her heels, passing the cheering yellow crowd a second time as she crossed the line, the long white ribbon falling before her. The prolonged roar from the Nightingale crowd reassured her that Annie had indeed come second.

Judy felt herself being lifted onto the shoulders of her friends and lost herself in the ecstasy of victory. She was carried towards the platform where prizes were to be given out and was set down carefully on the grass. There was nothing about Miss Miller's face to suggest anger or disappointment; she gave her professional smile, wholly appropriate and wholly insincere, as Judy climbed the steps and crossed the platform towards her, lowering her head to receive her medal. Miss Miller's smile remained fixed as she draped the gold medal around Judy's neck and shook her hand, whispering as she did, "Dirty little Jew. I knew I couldn't trust you."

Judy staggered off the platform, troubled by a discordant whistling in her ears. As she walked back to the pavilion, she heard a voice behind her. "Judy? Jude, whatever's the matter?" It was Annie at her side with that incriminating silver medal around her neck. Judy felt her friend's arm around her waist. "You don't look well. Let me find my mother."

"I have to get back to the track," Judy managed to say. "I've other races to run."

"Not for a while yet. Come and get a glass of water." Judy felt her body shuddering and swallowed a sob a little too late. "It's all right; you've just got a little wrung out.

Don't think I've ever seen you run so fast. You gave me quite a chase!"

"Annie? Can I tell you something?" Judy murmured. "Before we get to the tent?"

"What's up?"

"Promise you won't tell anyone else? Not another soul?"

"Cross my heart and hope to die."

∿

"Mary, are you absolutely sure that's what she said?" demanded Mr Peterson, looking in astonishment at his wife across the room. He had taken to doing his marking in the small staff room Miss Miller had set aside for Harry Forbes, largely to keep the poor man company, and had arrived back at the cottage to find dinner concluded and cleared away and his daughters in their rooms doing their prep. "I find that very difficult to believe, even from that woman!"

"Ask Annie yourself if you're not sure, but it sounds perfectly plausible to me. Would you really put it past Elsa Miller to say a thing like that?"

Peterson gave a weary shrug and sat down at the dining table, which was empty except for a glass of water and a covered dinner plate. It was the sort of evening when he would have loved to have sat outside in their little garden, but since it was in view of the school, he could never be sure that he was not being gawped at by small numbers of nosy girls. "She might think it perhaps," he conceded. "She has always been notoriously anti-Semitic. But to say that to a girl's face?"

"Darling, it's hard to believe, but it's far harder to imagine Judy making up such a story. We've come to know her so well over the years. I can't quite imagine her lying about such a thing."

Peterson plucked up the courage to uncover his dinner and was quietly impressed. Mary had made plump little rounds of potato and sausage meat with some boiled carrots at the side. "Did the vegetables come from the garden?" he asked.

"Yes, Lucy dug them up for me before school. I asked her about it."

"Judy?" he asked, his mind still on the carrots.

"No, Miss Miller."

"You did what?"

"No need to go into a blind panic," Mary reassured him. "I don't mean about the comment. I asked her if she had told Judy to let Annie win. She admitted she had, because she felt that it was unfair to Annie that she always came second. She also thought it unhealthy for Judy to win too often." Mary sat down opposite her husband. "I can't say I approve of her fixing the race like that. Annie has never complained about coming second to Judy, and it's hardly fair to make a girl perform below par. Sport is competitive; children need to know that." She hesitated long enough to prompt her husband to look up at her. "A nasty thought occurred to me, darling."

"What?"

"I wondered, since she said that beastly thing to Judy . . . well, what if she didn't want Judy to win an important race because she looks like a Jew? Annie's blonde; she looks . . . well, she looks—"

"Mary, Judy is not Jewish!" Peterson remonstrated. "She's a practising Catholic. We take her to Mass! I don't under-

37

stand why Judy has started making such a fuss about all this; she never used to so much as mention it. Now she's going around with a star around her neck. It's absurd!''

"It's hardly surprising when you think of what's happening to the Jews in Germany. I think she's being very brave, for what it's worth. If your own people were suffering . . .'' Mary trailed off, swallowing the end of the sentence. "I'm sorry.''

Peterson was staring intently at the edge of the table, the meal forgotten. "She's not doing herself any good, brooding over such a tenuous link with the past. She may come to regret it, the way things are going. If the Germans invade . . .''

"Do you think they will?''

"The war's going badly in France; it's an open secret,'' said Peterson. "And if France falls, we all know where Hitler will turn his attention. These girls are my responsibility, Mary, all of them, but Judy's the only one I truly worry about. She can't keep her head down.''

Mary got up and stood behind her husband, gently massaging his shoulders. "She's only a child, darling. No one's going to come for her, even if there is an invasion.''

"She's sixteen. She's old enough to be sent to a camp.'' He said the word as though it were an obscenity and found it impossible to say anything else. The room descended into uneasy silence.

"You don't know what's going to happen,'' said Mary at last, but she could feel his body juddering with the effort of keeping calm. "Please try not to think about it too much. It's not good for you.''

"I know,'' he said softly, still not daring to look at her.

"It's just . . . I've had to stop walking near the beach in the morning. All that wire . . . all that wire everywhere. I keep seeing all those dead faces."

Mary sat down beside him, taking his hands in hers. "Darling, your time for fighting is over. This isn't your war. Now, you just concentrate on the school. Who knows, I might be making too much of this anyway."

"No, I think there might be something in it," said Peterson, grasping her hands like a lifeline. "I'll keep half an eye on Judy just in case. Frankly, I always do. Someone has to."

4

The week that followed was a bad one for the world, but the girls were kept blissfully sheltered from the news of the Dutch surrender and its grim implications for the rest of western Europe, with even Judy struggling to find out what was going on. She had enough troubles of her own to contend with, having comprehensively failed to perform Miss Miller's painless little task. It had been so beastly, she mused as she lay awake four nights in succession, distracted by the snores and murmurs of the dormitory. Trying to force her to lose like that. It was worse than stopping her from running or banning her from sports day altogether. She would have been devastated. But to make her *lose*?

Dirty little Jew . . . The strange thing was that the insult had almost reassured her once she had recovered from the shock. It had a ring of affirmation about it. It proved her own belief that Miss Miller was an evil villain, but it was so much more than that. In a peculiar way, Miss Miller knew who she really was—she accepted that she was a Jew, even if that made her a disgusting creature to be attacked at every possible moment. Miss Miller, vile woman that she was, did not sit her down and patiently explain to her that she was making a fuss about nothing, that one Jewish grandparent counted for nothing, that this was just a passing silliness she really ought to have grown out of by now. The fact that

Miss Miller hated her was a grave misfortune, but it was infinitely more satisfying than being hated for being clumsy or untidy or perpetually late. Miss Miller's anti-Semitism was an initiation into the adult world of politics and visceral tribalism; it was the sort of hatred adults felt for one another, not the annoyance they exuded towards mere children.

There was, of course, a drawback, as Judy had already discovered in life, and that was that being violently loathed by one's headmistress was never going to be a comfortable or particularly safe affair, whatever the cause. It was at least part of the reason she had written a letter to her father, begging him to send for her and to find her some gainful employment assisting the war effort. She knew she should be back in London, where the real drama of the war was sure to take place. Judy was mature enough to know that the gleeful whispers and prophecies of doom from the girls were childishly morbid—none of them truly wanted Jerry to turn up in tanks on their doorstep—but nevertheless, she had some sense that she was alive in extraordinary times and that she might miss her appointment with history if she could not get her piece of the action before it was all over.

That and the need to get away from Miss Miller, whom she had avoided ever since their encounter on sports day. Nothing had happened, in spite of Miss Miller's threat that Judy would regret returning to school. She had failed to obey an instruction, and nothing had happened. She would have liked to believe that it had been an empty threat, the sort of thing one of the less experienced teachers might blurt out in a temper without having any intention of carrying out: "Interrupt again, Miss Randall, and I'll throw you out of the window!" But Miss Miller was not given to saying anything she did not mean, and she was patient enough to bide her time if necessary. *Beware the wrath of a patient woman . . .*

Judy's father had sent a response to her plea by return of post. The letter was curt and to the point, taking up a whole six inches of notepaper. She was to stop being a blithering idiot, complete her education and leave grown men to deal with the war. She had read the letter over breakfast, shortly before a prefect arrived at her side like the ghost of Caesar to say that she was expected in Miss Miller's study at the start of morning break. Her heart sank like a dead herring. It was payback time, and she had nearly two hours to agonise over the possibilities.

~

The thud of the wooden blackboard duster landing squarely on her desk jolted Judy back to life. "Wakey-wakey, Judy!" exclaimed Mr Forbes, marching towards her to reclaim it. "Not like you to daydream."

"Missed," she replied, wiping the chalk dust off her lips.

"I was not intending to hit you; I was aiming for the desk. I never miss, I assure you." He held out a piece of chalk to her. "Let's see what you can make of the problem."

Judy would ordinarily have been delighted to jump onto the teacher's platform and impress the class with the speed at which she could find the solution. She particularly liked it when she was timed or raced the class to find the answer, but today she was too distracted by whatever Miss Miller was planning and could not concentrate on her lesson. She stepped onto the platform with the queasiness of a child in trouble and looked warily up at the blackboard. It was the first time she understood the torment nonmathematicians must go through when put on the spot: all she could see was a dizzying blur of numbers and signs, with no obvious coherence at all. Not only could she not calculate the answer, she had absolutely no idea how to begin.

"I'm so sorry, sir, but I don't feel frightfully well this morning," she said, clutching her head for effect. Judy tried to gauge the response of the rest of the class without turning to look, hoping against all hope that she might win some sympathy.

Mr Forbes took the chalk back and marched her in the direction of the door. "Get yourself a glass of water," he said, following her out into the corridor to avoid speaking within earshot of the other girls.

"You'd better pull yourself together, Judy. You can't face her like that."

"You know, don't you?" whispered Judy, desperately trying to ignore the sensation of her heart thumping against her ribs. "She's called in all the teachers! What on earth am I supposed to have done?"

Mr Forbes inclined his head to one side, as though he found her denial disappointingly childish. "Come on now, Judy, she's found the money you stole. Now go and calm yourself down, please. You've not got long."

⁓

When Peterson had arrived in the school building after breakfast and been told the news by his wife, his first thought had been to try to find Judy to ask her what on earth was going on. Unfortunately, he was a little on the last minute, as ever, and was not due to teach her class until the afternoon. By the time he caught sight of Judy, he was already seated with the other teachers in Miss Miller's study, with his wife glancing anxiously at him from the opposite side and Harry Forbes fidgeting maddeningly next to him.

As soon as Judy stepped into the room, Peterson knew she had been informed somehow or other about the accusation. There was no look of bewilderment or hesitation on her face whatsoever as she surveyed the people in the room—a detail that might easily be used against her—and she walked with a firm, almost determined air about her. The normal protocol was that when a girl got herself into very serious trouble, the teachers were summoned and informed of the offence beforehand, but the girl concerned received no warning that she was to have an audience when she stepped into Miss Miller's study. Either her informant suspected that the accusation was false and had made the decision to forewarn her or was too new to understand the rules.

"I think you know why you have been called here," began Miss Miller, standing before them as though she were addressing Parliament. Her presentation had a well-worn feel to it and had been used over and over across the years to intimidate miscreants of all ages, but Judy had never managed to get herself into quite such hot water before and had never heard the speech. She was undoubtedly frightened but was challenging herself not to let it show; yet Peterson could see that she was clenching her teeth and holding her hands behind her back to stop herself trembling.

"I have no idea, Miss Miller," answered Judy, a little more quietly than was usual for her.

45

"Speak up. I can hardly hear you!"

"I said I have no idea," repeated Judy a shade louder, with the slightest shred of temper creeping in already. "What have I done?"

"I do not like liars any more than I like thieves," answered Miss Miller, looking the girl squarely in the eye. The presentation was over, her remarks were addressed entirely to one person, and the rest of them were consigned immediately to the role of hapless spectators. "Why did you steal the tuck-shop cashbox? Were you intending to run away perhaps?"

Judy made no attempt at sounding surprised. "I did no such thing. I would never steal so much as a boiled sweet."

"Don't waste my time, my girl. The cashbox was found in your bedside locker. You were not quite caught red-handed, but near enough for me."

Peterson could feel the sweat gathering at the back of his neck, just under the inner seam of his collar. He suspected that Harry Forbes (it was so obviously him, by a quick process of deduction) had unwittingly done Judy a disservice by giving her time to prepare a defence. If she had been caught off guard, she might well have gone to pieces and simply accepted whatever sentence fell on her in the absence of a ready alternative. As things stood, however, she had had time to steel herself and was all the more likely to be troublesome.

"Miss Miller," said Judy as calmly as she could manage—but her voice quavered in spite of herself—"if I were cunning enough to steal a cashbox from the tuckshop, under the noses of the prefects, do you really think I would be foolish enough to hide it somewhere as obvious as that?"

Faced with Miss Miller's cold glare, Judy turned to the teachers as though seeking out a protector. "I didn't do it!" she protested, more forcefully this time. "I'm a respectable girl. You know I would never steal a penny!"

Peterson could feel his wife's eyes boring into him, willing him to intervene, but it was Harry Forbes who stood up and shuffled quietly towards Judy. "I think it would be best if you just owned up," he said kindly, placing a conciliatory hand on her arm. "No one will think the less of you if you say you're sorry and take the consequences."

"But I didn't do it!" she almost shouted, backing away from him as though he had personally betrayed her, which in a way he had. "I am not a thief! I will not own up to something I didn't do!"

"Judy, Judy, this is wrong," continued Forbes in the same gentle, considerate tone that Peterson knew would infuriate Judy all the more. He was behaving in every sense like a benevolent father addressing an errant daughter he still believes in but who is trying his patience. The approach might have worked if Forbes did not look about twelve and Judy were not so implacable. "It really would be a lot better for you if you took it like a big girl. It's not nice to make a scene, now, is it?"

"I did not do it!" Judy barked at him in slow staccato, clenching her fists so tightly she looked to all intents and purposes as though she wanted to thump him.

"Just hold out your hands, and in a minute it will be over and we can all forget it ever happened."

"Thank you, Mr Forbes," came a terse voice from the direction of Miss Miller, who evidently did not appreciate another person taking centre stage. "Why don't you sit down?" She waited for him to shuffle back awkwardly to his seat, all the while looking anxiously in Judy's direction as though begging her to do the right thing. Miss Miller turned her attention back to Judy. "I've had enough of this. If you refuse to cooperate with me, I shall have no alternative but to have you expelled."

That was the moment Peterson knew beyond doubt that Miss Miller had set up this whole situation. For reasons known only to herself—perhaps Judy was right, perhaps it was pure and simple anti-Semitism—Elsa Miller wanted her out of the way, but finding a reason to expel a child whose worst offence had been a supper protest would have looked suspicious. By creating a situation in which she appeared to be giving Judy a chance to make amends for a wicked act, and Judy refusing, Miss Miller could appear perfectly professional and Judy would effectively expel herself in front of her teachers. Miss Miller knew—as Peterson knew, and some of the others must surely have known—that Judy would never admit to a crime she had not committed, and still less would she submit to a caning on account of it. A nervier or more pragmatic girl might, but Judy was neither, and she would never be able to bring herself to go through with it.

Miss Miller took hold of Judy's arm, but she snatched it away and stepped back between the rows of teachers. Peterson was suddenly aware that, in spite of her relatively small stature, Judy was a good couple of inches taller than her headmistress and in considerably better physical shape. Never in his entire teaching career had he seen a pupil go into open revolt like this, but if he could not persuade Judy to back down, the situation could easily turn nasty. "Judith Jane Randall, I am giving you thirty seconds to pull yourself together and come over here," said Miss Miller, in the coldly aggressive tone they all recognised. "If you are expelled from this school for stealing, you can be certain you will not be taken by any other school. If you are willing to throw away your education out of infantile pride, that is your misfortune."

Judy stood where she was, glancing at them one by one in silent accusation. Peterson knew she was weighing up the consequences in her mind and was slowly appreciating the trap in which she had been caught. She had a bright future ahead of her and a father wealthy enough to support her through Oxford and perhaps even an academic position one day. However much Judy might resent being at school, she was no fool and had to know how much she stood to lose if she were expelled. And yet in the heat of the moment . . .

"You are all cowards!" shouted Judy, so explosively that a few of them flinched. "You know perfectly well I didn't steal anything, you *cowards*!"

"Judy, that's enough!"

Judy glared in Miss Miller's direction in undisguised contempt and walked slowly towards her, stamping her feet with every step. Peterson felt his wife's eyes burning him again and knew he would never be able to forgive himself if he did not get up now. In a second the decision was made; he rose to his feet and hurried forward, nudging Judy very gently to one side. "I'm sorry; I cannot let this happen. This is wrong."

Miss Miller looked at him in disbelief. There was an agonised pause of five eternal seconds before she found her voice: "Have you taken leave of your senses?"

He was aware of the dangerousness of the situation, but he could not sit down again now. "I in no way wish to question your judgement, madam, and if Judy had stolen that cashbox, you would be quite right to punish her. But this makes no sense. I doubt anyone in this room honestly believes she stole anything."

"The evidence was found in her locker," answered Miss Miller quietly. "I think we have already established that much. Short of catching her in the act of stealing, I'm not sure how much more evidence you could need."

Peterson heard a rustle of skirts behind him, and Matron appeared at his side. "Perhaps some other girl put it there?" suggested Matron, in a breathless voice. "It's a big dormitory, and plenty of girls come and go during the day. Judy has been under my care since she was seven years old. I simply do not believe she would have done this."

There were more footsteps. Mrs Peterson and finally Harry Forbes had risen to their feet, and the four of them stood in an awkward group facing Miss Miller, who squared up to them with admirable authority. "Is this mutiny?" she enquired, looking to Peterson for an explanation as the obvious ringleader.

"Not at all," Peterson assured her. He turned to face the others, indicating that they should sit down to avoid the appearance of ganging up. The tension in the room ebbed just a little. Peterson knew he had broken an important rule of professional etiquette by breaking ranks and had to put things right as far as possible. "Judy, come here, please." Judy had gratefully removed herself to the far corner of the room and approached him with the utmost reluctance, not quite trusting that the situation would not turn against her again. "Tell me honestly, what are the reasons for which you are most often in trouble?"

"Sir . . ."

"There's no need to be shy. Just answer the question. What have you done over the past year to get yourself into trouble?"

Judy reddened. "Well, untidiness, lateness, er . . ."

"Forgetfulness!" called out a voice from the back of the room. It was Miss Gibbs, the needlework teacher, prompting a welcome patter of laughter. "Lost and forgotten pins, needles, thimbles . . ."

"Yes, forgetfulness," Judy interrupted, shifting her weight from one foot to the other. "Is this really necessary, sir?"

"It is absolute necessary, I'm afraid. Anything else?"

"I'm a Roman Catholic—we tend to make our confessions privately."

"Anything *else*?"

"Does the pet mouse in the lacrosse cupboard count?"

More laughter. "Yes, it most certainly does. And let's leave the small matter of the food strike, shall we?" Peterson turned back to Miss Miller, who was still glancing tonelessly in his direction, every muscle in her face taut to breaking point. "You are quite right to take this seriously, and if after further investigation it becomes clear that only Judy could have stolen that cashbox, she must of course make amends for what she has done. But does it seem likely that a pupil who has only ever been punished for the most trivial of reasons would suddenly—at the age of sixteen—take it upon herself to do something so shameful? I think we may have to consider that someone else committed this offence and tried to pin the blame on her. It would hardly be the first time."

Miss Miller took a moment to put her thoughts in order before responding. "You are quite right, Mr Peterson. I will take on this little investigation myself and see where it leads."

"I am quite happy to—"

"I will take it on myself. It is only right and proper that I should do so. I think that should close the matter for now."

As Judy and the teachers filed out, Peterson felt a wearisome anxiety sweeping over him again. He could not have put his suspicion into words, but he had a sense that invisible battle lines had been drawn and that he and his wife and Forbes and Matron had found themselves on the wrong side.

~

Elsa Miller sat down and stared at the desk before her until her eyes began to blur with the effort. She had developed the habit of mentally retreating from the world around her whenever she was struggling to cope with a situation, a form of self-defence she had learnt in a far-harsher school than this in some distant nightmare of childhood. She was slipping carefully away from the now-empty room, blocking out the incriminating sight of the scratched metal cashbox she had personally removed from the tuckshop and that she had compelled another child to plant in the dormitory. It had been a clumsy, shabby thing to do, however she reworked the story to please her nagging conscience, the sort of action she would have thought disgusting if she had caught a child framing another to get her unjustly punished.

Of course, Judy's response had been characteristically disgraceful, a sure sign of bad breeding. That raised voice, those ludicrous histrionics, the like of which Elsa had never seen in thirty years of teaching. The girl might be capable of running faster than an Aryan, but her intemperate display had proved her inferiority beyond any reasonable doubt, as had the devious way she had manipulated her teachers into taking her part. It had been a mistake to employ a married couple in the first place; if Peterson expressed an opinion, his wife would obviously do as he told her without a second thought, and poor barren Matron could be expected to behave as though every child in the establishment were hers.

Of course, it was wrong of her to despise the girl because of what she was, and Elsa was not even sure she knew precisely what it was about Judy that got her hackles up so badly; but she had never been able to hide her disdain for the child, even when Judy was very much younger. She was an honest-enough woman to admit to herself that she actively looked for reasons to be offended or enraged by Judy, and if a teacher looked hard enough, he would always find some justification for reprimanding a child. It was hardly as though Judy could help her lineage even if it damned her, and Elsa recognized that she ought to be emotionally detached from the girl. The struggle for racial purity was a harsh necessity; it was nothing personal. After all, Judy as such was not to blame for having no meaningful purpose in the new world order, and she was too young to see herself

53

as anything other than singularly important. It would take time and perhaps a little pain for a girl as privileged as Judy to accept her new position in society, but she would have to accept it. When the Germans arrived . . .

Elsa felt an unnerving burning about the eyes and tried to blur her vision again, but the empty room revealed itself in a hundred sharp lines and unforgiving details. It was a room where she was always alone, even when it was full of people. Perhaps that was all it was, this ugly descent into misery and resentment and not a little fear. Nothing more sinister than the slow encroachment of the years every man and woman has to face. Even those ridiculous girls in their tunics and pinafores and straw hats, those pampered, empty-headed creatures who thought themselves hard done by if there was no cake for supper and who believed a cold shower constituted suffering. They would all suffer this fate eventually, the torment of facing the mirror every morning, the aching of joints, the sapping of energy, that struggle to find one's place in a world forever on the march. Was it reasonable to despise those girls for the youth they would lose one day without even noticing?

This was self-pity, Elsa reproached herself, another unattractive sign of age. She knew that there were girls in her care who had truly suffered, if not as much as she fondly imagined her own generation had suffered—Isobel Langridge had been sent home only last term because her brother had been killed in France. Elsa had received the telegram from Isobel's father, but it had been Matron who had broken the news to little Isobel, wiped away her tears, packed her trunk and seen her off at the station. There were bound to be many more if Parliament did not see sense and negotiate a peace.

Many more telegrams, many more girls left without fathers and brothers. By rights, those unsuspecting girls ought to be deserving of her sympathy, but it had been a long time since her heart had stirred with any tender emotion whatsoever.

Enough! Elsa rose to her feet, drumming her fists against the desk before walking the three brisk steps to the window. Nothing had happened in this room that was worth brooding over. A poorly thought-out plan had been thwarted—*she* had been thwarted—by an interfering man who thought a little too highly of himself. A tiresome girl had temporarily slipped the net. That was all. She would not grace the incident with more of her attention than it honestly deserved. Elsa quickly determined the best course of action—let it all go quiet for a few days; tell Peterson that she remained suspicious that Judy was the culprit, but in the absence of clearer evidence, it would be best to drop the matter.

She glanced across the gardens in the direction of the lawn that sloped down to the Petersons' cottage. Elsa squinted, searching the area for any sign of human activity, but she was satisfied that no member of the family could have gone home at this time. Both the adults would be teaching now, and the girls would be hard at work if they knew what was good for them. She picked up her summer coat and hat, paused to pick up her bag and stepped out into the quiet corridor.

5

Somewhere between Judy's fight against false accusations and her first dalliance with criminal activity, Belgium fell, the British Expeditionary Force was gloriously evacuated from Dunkirk, and the Nazis bombed Paris. Apart from these considerations, life at Mulwith slipped into the daily rhythm of early morning runs, cold showers, dull and duller lessons and ever-deteriorating food, which the kitchens blamed on Adolf Hitler.

Judy, in the meantime, was a woman on a mission. The young are innocent enough to retain a powerful sense of justice, and Judy was particularly afflicted. She was certain now that Miss Miller was a Jew hater; the attempt to label her a thief had been a clumsy act of revenge over that ridiculous sports day stunt, even if she could never have persuaded anyone else that the old witch herself was behind it. Matron and Mr Forbes were sure another girl had it in for her, but Judy knew better, and all that remained now was for her to prove it.

"I'm sure you're right," said Annie as they lay on the rug in Annie's bedroom, listening to gramophone records. "But oughtn't you to drop the matter really?"

Annie had that uncertain tone she always used when she was sure Judy was completely in the wrong but could not quite bring herself to come out and say it. Judy took a deep breath in place of an answer, equally unwilling to start an argument when she was having such a good time. She loved Annie's room, a spacious converted loft tucked cosily away under the cottage roof, with eaves cupboards and wooden beams crossing the ceiling that managed to make the room feel more intimate than it really was. Without the opposite windows open, the heat up there would have been unbearable, but a pleasing draught rippled through the room that day, carrying with it the faintest sounds of birdsong and the scent of roses in their first bloom under the window ledge.

The gramophone did not belong to Annie—it really belonged downstairs—but the senior Petersons were having a cup of tea with Mr Forbes, and the girls were under strict instructions to stay well out of the way. The gramophone had the adult advantage of keeping the girls occupied (or so they fondly imagined) whilst also drowning out the enticing drone of staff room gossip circulating in the kitchen. The latter was less important, as Annie and Judy were perfectly distracted by their own exchange of school gossip. "The trouble is, Jude, she might just be beastly. You know what old spinsters are like. I shall get married as soon as ever I can, to make absolutely sure I do not to turn into that."

Judy giggled mischievously. She felt that she knew exactly which poor unfortunate Annie Peterson had her eye on, and he was seated at the kitchen table at that very second. Half the girls in the school had a pash on Mr Forbes. It was inevitable that a young man with dreamy blue eyes and soft curls like a Greek god should become the hero of every romantic schoolgirl's imagination; and the limp gave him a faintly tragic air, as though he were a wounded soldier. Miss

Miller, perhaps anticipating the risk she had taken in hiring such a one, appeared to have gone to considerable lengths to isolate him not just from the girls but also from the rest of the teaching staff, creating a male staff room for just two men and initiating so many new rules and regulations that Judy wondered that the man did not flee in the middle of the night out of sheer desperation for contact with the rest of the human race.

"I think I have proof this time," said Judy in a low voice. She got up and replaced the record with a version of the 1812 Symphony, relishing the sense of mystery she was causing by making her friend wait until the music became ludicrously ear-splitting before going on. It was, of course, completely unnecessary to use the music to conceal what she was about to say, as the two girls had been lying close enough for her to whisper in Annie's ear, but the dramatic effect was more pronounced if she stood up. In any case, she needed to get the incriminating exhibit out of her bag, which she had slung on Annie's bed. "Take a look at this."

Judy brought out a book with the same flourish with which a magician might have pulled a rabbit out of a hat. "A book?" asked Annie, shouting above the music and immediately undermining the whole point of it. "So what?"

Judy gave a sigh Annie had heard many times over the years of their friendship and pointed to the title embossed on the front: *The Protocols of the Elders of Zion*. Annie looked up at her friend in weary confusion, knowing that the title ought to mean something desperately profound, but she had never seen the thing before in her entire life. She was not sure what she had expected Judy to pull out of the bag —a swastika armband, a signed photograph of the Führer perhaps—but a dreary little book with a boring name came as an anticlimax.

There was no time to explain. The door flew open, causing both girls to jump. Mrs Peterson was standing before them with a look of thunder on her face. She marched over to the gramophone and turned it off in one swift move. "What on earth is all this noise for?" she demanded, shaking her head in the maddening way adults do when they have had their worst suspicions proved correct and are positively delighted about it. "I should have known you'd disturb everyone if I let you take that thing upstairs. We can't hear ourselves think!"

"Sorry, Mrs Peterson, that was my fault," said Judy immediately. "I had forgotten how well the sound carries."

"What's that?" asked Mrs Peterson, pointing at the book Judy had been in the process of slipping back into her bag.

"It's only a book I was showing Annie," said Judy. "I borrowed it."

"Yes," Annie chimed in. "*The Protocols of the* . . . sorry, Judy, what was the title again?"

Mrs Peterson flinched almost invisibly. "The what?"

"Nothing," said Judy.

"*The Protocols of Zion*," said Annie, cheerfully.

Mrs Peterson held out her hand, opening and closing her fingers to indicate that she expected Judy to hand over the book at once. Judy's shoulders drooped; she suppressed the urge to glare at her friend for being such an unspeakable sneak and handed the book to Mrs Peterson. "I find it very hard to believe that you could be recommending such a book to your friend," said Mrs Peterson calmly, looking back at Judy with a half smile, "and I should like to know from whom you have borrowed it. It is hardly from the school library now, is it?"

Judy lowered her eyes, knowing that every second she delayed giving an answer only incriminated her further. "I wasn't recommending it; I . . . I found it."

"Oh? Where?"

But Judy could not bear to answer. This was the one danger of a friendship with a teacher's child: the world of adult interference and rules and discipline was never far away, even in a family home. "It's only a book, Mummy," Annie cried, aware that she had let her friend down somehow, without intending to do so. Annie could have said anything —*Moby Dick*, *Great Expectations*, *The Adventures of Sherlock Holmes*. But even getting the title of the thing wrong had caused a disaster, and she did not understand why. It was unlike her mother to be so shocked and angry. Neither girl knew how to rescue the situation.

"If you won't tell me, I think you had better come downstairs, Judy," said Mrs Peterson at last, turning to leave the room with the book still clasped in one hand. "Annie, you will stay in your room."

As Judy shuffled miserably out of the room, she turned back to look at Annie, who was frantically mouthing the words "Sorry! Sorry! Sorry!"

But it was Judy who felt sorry. More than the fear she felt gnawing at the pit of her stomach, as she stepped down the wooden spiral staircase and onto the landing and down the main stairs, she felt the aching sense that she was about to ruin the afternoon for everyone. The dining room looked so blissfully familial as they entered, the air still cloudy with fruity smoke from the men's pipes, but Mr Peterson and

Mr Forbes stopped talking as soon as they saw the look on Mary's face. Mr Forbes instinctively rose to his feet at the entrance of two females, then remembered himself and sat down again, looking at Judy for an explanation.

Mary put the book down heavily in front of her husband. She did not sit down at the table herself and did not invite Judy to sit either. It was the first time Judy had ever been deliberately made to feel uneasy in that house, and she could not bring herself to look at any of them. "Judy has brought in some interesting reading," said Mary curtly, indicating the title in case the two men had failed to notice it.

Peterson groaned and shook his head, giving Judy a supercilious look that was curiously reassuring. "Oh, Judy, for goodness' sake! Whatever would you be wanting with this rubbish? Is this your idea of knowing your enemy?"

"In a way," said Judy awkwardly. "I was trying—" She was prevented from finishing her sentence by Mary rapping on the table.

"It's not hers, if that's what you imagine," said Mary. "Open it."

Peterson opened the book at the title page. "Elsa Miller" and "November 1921" were written in neat, formal handwriting across the top. The pages were curled from having been thumbed through many times. "Judy, would it be indiscreet of me to ask how you got hold of this?"

"I found it," she said in a small voice.

"Speak up!"

"I found it," she said more strongly.

"You stole it, you mean."

"I didn't steal it!" she protested, finding what she imagined to be some safe ground. "I said I found it!"

"Don't raise your voice to me!"

"You told me to speak up!"

Upstairs, he thought he could hear his daughter's muffled sobs and he looked desperately at his wife for assistance. Wordlessly, Mary slipped out of the room to deal with Annie, leaving Judy without a much-needed mediator.

Peterson placed his head in his hands. He could feel the beginnings of a headache; the happy, relaxed lunch and idle afternoon were slipping away into distant memory. "What do you mean, you found it?" he said, with as much calmness as he could muster.

"She left it next to the post tray. She put down some things she was holding so that she could rummage through the post. There was a letter she seemed especially pleased about, and she went off with it in such a hurry that she forgot about her other things. I think the letter may have been—"

"Judy," he said severely, "you are getting a little old to play at spying on your teachers, don't you think?"

"She may not have been spying," Forbes put in, generously. He had not yet lost the habit of giving humanity the benefit of the doubt—a few more years of teaching would no doubt remedy that impairment—and Judy was the sort of person who effortlessly encouraged men to come to her rescue. "It was hardly the girl's fault if she happened to pass the post tray when Miss Miller was checking for letters."

Peterson treated Judy to the same snide half smile Mary had so recently given her. "Were you, dear? Were you just passing when you happened to stumble upon Miss Miller off her guard?"

63

Judy looked at the two men, the younger waiting desperately for her to affirm his good opinion of her, the older awaiting the inevitable. "She hates me, sir! She called me a dirty little Jew—"

"Judy, I think I may have told you once or twice before to let that comment pass," repeated Peterson. "It's unseemly to bear a grudge. Has she repeated the remark or anything like it since?"

"No, but she clearly hates me." Judy tried to justify herself, but she knew she sounded like an obsessive little girl with a bee in her bonnet about a woman who had punished her once too often. "She's harsher with me than with the others. There's something about the way she talks to me. Doesn't the book prove something? Why should she possess a book like that and carry it about with her?"

Peterson stood up with the weariness of a man who has been forced out of bed in the middle of the night to investigate a noise downstairs. "It's certainly suspicious," he conceded, "but hardly conclusive. I'm afraid that this book has sold many copies all over the world. Those who take its claims seriously may not be very nice people, but it hardly makes her a Nazi sympathiser, if that is what you are trying to prove. And it does not hide the fact that you stole a book that does not belong to you."

"I didn't steal it; I only wanted to show it to someone," she said desperately, but the energy was trickling out of her so fast she could hardly bring herself to speak at all. "I was going to show it to you."

"You didn't, though, did you? You knew, I suspect, that I would be unimpressed. Did you have any intention of returning it?"

Judy shook her head. "I suppose not. I needed to keep it as evidence."

"Then you are a thief. It's a poor way to pay back those of us who believed in you when you were accused of stealing something else."

"I did not steal that cashbox, sir! You know I didn't! That's only a book. It was there for the taking."

"And if her purse had been left there for the taking, would you have taken it? Come on now, I expected better of you than this."

"I'm sorry."

Judy sat down absentmindedly, more from exhaustion than anything else. "Get up. I did not invite you to sit down."

The deliberate humiliation proved too much for Judy, and her eyes swam with tears.

She was startled by a hand squeezing hers. It was Forbes, who had taken advantage of his temporary invisibility from the conversation to move round to where she was standing. "This does seem unduly harsh," he said, assuming the role of the seasoned diplomat. "The book is very incriminating —let's face it—and Miss Miller is needlessly heavy-handed with some of the girls; I've seen it for myself."

"Step away from her, Harry," said Peterson, without looking at either of them. "There's a good chap."

Forbes snatched his hand away from Judy's hand as though he had scalded himself. "I was only trying to—"

"Judy, you will return the book to Miss Miller immediately. Whatever else it is, it is not yours."

"You can't ask her to do that!" exclaimed Forbes, regarding him in astonishment. He knew perfectly well that the

Petersons had a strained relationship with the headmistress at the best of times, whereas they treated Judy like one of their own. They must have covered for her dozens of times over the years, but now Peterson seemed determined to deliver the girl's head on a plate. And all over a copy of a disgusting book Peterson would have tossed on the fire given half a chance.

Peterson's eyes flashed with anger, a sight so rare Judy instinctively moved towards the door. "I most certainly can ask her to return a book to its rightful owner. I'll thank you not to interfere."

"I'll return it," Forbes volunteered. "I'll say I found it lying around and realised it was hers. She won't suspect anything that way." Peterson did not move. "Would that put everything right?"

Peterson nodded slowly. "I don't suppose it serves any good purpose to make her suffer more than she needs to." He was saving face, but Peterson's only concern at that moment was to stop himself looking like a man who had backed the wrong horse: he knew that Elsa Miller was still furious about their public confrontation and would use this little misdemeanour to hurt him far more than Judy. He turned to Judy. "You listen to me, my girl. You are to stay well away from Miss Miller. Do you understand?"

"Yes." She hesitated. "Yes, sir."

"Whatever ridiculous notions you are nursing about Miss Miller, you are to drop them immediately. Stay well away from her: no more snooping, no more spying and certainly no more stealing or gathering of evidence, if that's what you wish to call it. If you know what's good for you, you'll put your head down and get on with your work like the others."

Judy opened her mouth to speak, but no sound came out. She nodded lamely.

"You will write out two hundred times 'I must not steal.' Leave the lines on my desk by the end of today. Now, I think you had better leave."

Judy's degradation was complete. It was far worse than being thrown out of class—which had happened many times before. She felt more as though she were being thrown out of the room by her own father. She was a small child again, being sent to her room for spoiling a family party.

As soon as Judy had fled the house, choking back tears, the two men were left free to argue uninterrupted. "I fail to see why you put her through so much over a book someone left lying around," Forbes began. "There was no real harm done."

"It was foolish," answered Peterson, reaching into his pocket for a badly needed cigarette, but his case had gone walkabouts. "Judy's not stupid. Miller does have her knife in her, but that only means she needs to behave better than the others, not worse. If she's forced out of the school, it will be very bad for her. She has nowhere else to go."

"Has she no family?"

"Her mother died some years ago—cancer, I believe. Her father is adamant that she is not to return to London."

Forbes took a cigarette case out of his pocket and offered it to Peterson by way of an olive branch. He helped himself gratefully. "I'm sorry if I spoke out of turn. I wasn't expecting you to come down on her so hard."

Peterson distracted himself lighting the cigarette. "You have to understand, Forbes, she's like a member of my family. Annie adopted her within weeks of her arrival. She's always in and out of this house during their free time. It makes it a little awkward when I have to discipline her. I can't seem to be giving her special treatment. I suppose that does mean I'm harsher than I need to be, but it's as much for her sake as mine." He took several short puffs on the cigarette, which Forbes found quite comical to watch. "Another thing, Harry, old man—keep your distance."

"From you?"

"From her. I saw the way you were looking at her."

Forbes blushed deeply. He could almost feel the redness creeping across his face, then over his neck and throat. "She's sixteen," he said.

"She's your pupil. Watch your step."

~

That evening, shortly before retiring for the night, Mr Peterson walked over to the school building and put his head round the door of the men's staff room. On his desk, as he had ordered, a pile of foolscap papers sat neatly, containing the words *I must not steal* in increasingly ragged handwriting, as Judy's frustration had waxed and waned. He could almost sense her exhaustion as the words became larger and farther apart with every line. There were two hundred of them at a quick count.

Peterson usually tore up the pages of lines in front of the child who had written them, as a final insult, but he could not quite bring himself to summon Judy before him for that particular pleasure when the day had gone so badly for her. He was about to tear them in half when he looked down and noticed an extra piece of paper folded into quarters, which had slipped onto the floor. He let the other pages fall undamaged into the wastepaper basket and picked it up. It was a letter from Judy.

Dear Mr Peterson,

I am so terribly sorry about the book. I know I should not have taken it away with me when Miss Miller left it near the post tray, and it would have been the decent thing to return it to her myself. Please do not be angry with Annie. She had nothing to do with it.

Please forgive me for ruining the afternoon. I feel awful about it.

With best wishes,
Judith Randall

Peterson knew that Judy was only attempting to be as formal and adult as possible, but her use of her full name to sign off the letter put him in mind of a door being slammed shut. He hoped he had not lost her trust at the one moment she most needed an authority figure to whom she could turn, and he pondered how best to let her know she was forgiven without getting her back up even further. Judy was too young to know it, but it was not safe for her to isolate herself. This was not the time to stand alone.

6

France had fallen and Britain stood alone. During those warm, languid, restless days as the summer term trickled away and the world trembled, Judy was left with a singular sense of becoming separated from the rest of humanity. A more mature mind observing her might have suggested that she was going through the predictable existential crisis so many youths experienced on the cusp of adulthood, that nagging sense of being different, misunderstood, the exception to the rule. No one likes to imagine that his plight is an expected and transient phase, but it was unlikely Judy would have accepted such a diagnosis even if there had been someone to talk things through with her.

She could not quite get her head around what was wrong exactly, but nothing was right with the world, even hers, and the more she mused on the wrongness of it all, the more she became convinced that she knew the reason. There was nothing wrong with the world of Mulwith School per se, apart from the fact that she was still living in it, which would perhaps explain her feeling of dislocation. She had outgrown it all, she told herself as she embarked on her morning run; her mind was on more important things, like Miss Miller's Nazi sympathies, and she could not be expected to focus her attention on anything more trivial.

It was hardly surprising, surely, that she had become a little careless with rules that belonged to a disappearing world.

With the Germans overrunning Europe, wreaking destruction as they went, how significant in the grand scheme of things was her lack of punctuality or her untidy hair or her trailing laces or her refusal to eat the blasted tripe stew they had served up for the third time last week?

But there was a more tangible problem, and it was this thought that troubled her the most as she focused her attention on the task at hand. Judy neared the Petersons' cottage and felt an all-too-familiar tug on her heart as the tumble-down building came into view. She would not admit it to herself, but every time she passed the cottage, a small part of her longed to run up the path and knock on the door; but things had become a little complicated since the book incident, and she had not entered the house since Mr Peterson had thrown her out. Her letter of apology had been duly accepted by way of a boiled sweet being pressed discreetly into her hand by Mrs Peterson at the end of the Monday afternoon games session and an assurance that the matter was closed, but she had had to decline an invitation to Sunday lunch due to finding herself in disgrace again—and then another invitation and another as she somehow managed to earn detentions faster than she could sit through them. The waters could close over quite quickly even on a long friendship, and Judy had finally suggested to Annie that they all give up on her altogether, an idea she had not expected Annie to accept quite so readily.

Then of course there had been the final outrage during last Friday afternoon's French class, which Judy suspected had put a permanent end to the Entente Cordiale between herself and the Peterson family. It galled her particularly badly because French was one of her favourite subjects, after mathematics and athletics. She spoke fluent French, thanks to her father packing her off to a convent near Poitiers for a month every summer for the past seven years—ever since the start of her mother's illness—and French lessons were the few occasions on which she was encouraged to be talkative. Prattling away on virtually any subject was regarded as educational.

But not on Friday. There had been something in the atmosphere that should have warned Judy to keep her mouth shut, but it may simply have been her own agitation colouring the way she saw everything. Thanks to being perpetually in trouble, Judy had found it impossible to catch Mr Peterson alone and had had no chance to discuss her latest suspicions with him. In the name of national security, she desperately needed to tell him that she had looked out of the window during a dull moment in a geography lesson and noticed Miss Miller slipping out of the school building in the direction of the village. She suspected he would say she was being silly again, but Judy was sure she had noticed her looking quite shifty as she walked away, checking over her shoulder and the like, exactly the way people do when they are up to no good.

"Judy, your turn," said Mr Peterson in French. He insisted upon speaking only French during his lessons, which the other girls found exhausting but which Judy planned to use as a cunning smokescreen. "You have two minutes to tell the class about the French novel you have chosen to study."

Judy stood up at her desk, paper in hand. "*The Three Musketeers* was written by Alexandre Dumas," she said as quickly as she could, deliberately gabbling the words to feign nervousness she had never experienced, "and was first published in serial form in 1844."

"Good, but please slow down, Judy."

She rushed on regardless. "The novel tells the story of D'Artagnan and his adventures when he goes to Paris from his rustic home to join the king's Musketeers."

"Slow down, dear; the rest of the class can't understand you."

"And the headmistress is a prostitute who is selling her country to the enemy. I saw her—" Judy and the rest of the class jumped at the sound of Mr Peterson's fist crashing against his desk. Judy froze as he advanced towards her. She made a split-second decision to try to continue in the hope he would forget what she had just said. "The main characters of the novel are Porthos, Athos and Aramis, D'Artagnan's companions . . ."

"What did you say?" asked Mr Peterson quietly. He was still speaking in French, but every girl in the room knew that Judy had said something terrible, even if it had been impossible to understand precisely what she had come out with.

Judy struggled to meet his gaze. He was so seldom angry in class that on the rare occasions he gave into it, no one quite knew what to expect. He had a habit, honed over many years of teaching, of concealing rage in a way that made the recipient only more frightened. His face would never betray a scowl or so much as a frown in moments like that. His expression would remain completely neutral, almost unreadable, whilst his eyes conveyed so much anger in a single, steady glance at the person in trouble that there could be no doubt in that person's mind that he had seriously overstepped the mark with him.

"The main characters of the story . . ." Judy tried to begin again, but she could feel her hands shaking around the moistening paper containing her prep, and she did not dare push him any further.

"You know perfectly well to what I am referring," he answered tonelessly. "Say it again just to make sure I am not going deaf in my old age."

Judy put down the paper and leant forward, pressing her hands down flat against her desk with the effort of holding her nerve. When she spoke, her words were quiet and rapid in the hope that only he would understand her. "The headmistress is a prostitute who—" She gave a strangled cry of pain as the ruler struck the back of her hand; she had been so distracted by the way he was looking at her that she had not even noticed what he was holding. There was a low murmur rippling across the room.

"Get out of my sight," he said, abruptly switching to English to make sure everyone knew the score. "I will not tolerate language like that about anyone, least of all a person entitled to your respect. You may count yourself grateful that I don't personally rinse your mouth out with soap. Now get out."

It had been no good telling him afterwards that she had substituted the word *putain* for "traitor" only because she had thought that the French word for a female traitor, *traîtresse*, was a little too obvious even to the class dunces, and she had not realised that the word she had chosen was quite that obscene. In the privacy of the men's staff room, without even the gentle presence of Mr Forbes to mediate, Mr Peterson's cold rage had been limitless. *Damnation without relief . . .*

Judy's unhappy thoughts were interrupted by the sound

of a gate opening with a protracted squeak, and Mrs Peterson appeared in her gym kit, jogging towards Judy in a way intended to suggest an unexpected meeting. Judy knew perfectly well, of course, that Mrs Peterson had been waiting for her to pass and had run out in time to intercept her. "Good morning, Judy!" she called, with forced brightness. "Glad to see you hard at it. Mind if I join you?"

"Why not?" answered Judy nonchalantly, though she was secretly delighted to have Mrs Peterson's undivided attention—or anybody's—for the first time in ages. "As long as you've not come to give me a telling off," she added. "I'm getting quite a lot of those at the moment. More than ever before."

Mrs Peterson got into rhythm next to Judy, matching her stride exactly. "Oh dear, you do seem to be getting into a lot of scrapes this term," she agreed. "Sorry we haven't seen much of you. What was the punishment for last Sunday?"

"Miss Gibbs said that I had rolled my eyes at her when she told me to do a silly job," said Judy.

"Come along, Judy, you know better than that!"

"But she *never* gives me lines! I would have expected a few sharp words, but I spent three hours writing out 'I must respect my elders'! Three *hours*!"

Mrs Peterson was apparently distracted by an invisible insect gnawing at the nape of her neck. "Well," she said cautiously, "perhaps she felt your impertinence had gone too far. She knows you hate lines more than anything else. I daresay she was trying to teach you a much-needed lesson."

There was no persuasive way Mrs Peterson could possibly have put that suggestion, and Judy felt a surge of anger sweeping over her like a sudden electrical charge. It caused her to power ahead, breaking all the rules of cross-country running by dashing into a sprint. "Everyone is teaching me a lesson!" she tried to shout, but breathlessness intervened. "Everyone! I can't breathe without someone pouncing on me and slapping some punishment on me! Or giving me extra work! I . . . I've ever so much extra maths to do for Mr Forbes!"

Judy staggered to a halt as suddenly as she had sprinted, fighting for breath as she did so; she grabbed wildly for some way to steady herself, staggered forward and ended up slumped against the nearest tree on her knees, panting idiotically.

"You're far too well trained to be making mistakes like that," said Mrs Peterson, taking the girl's arm. "Get up now."

"I can't breathe!" spluttered Judy, sinking her hands into the loamy soil. "I just can't—"

"You're hardly helping yourself, curling up like that. Get up!"

Judy scrambled to her feet whilst Mrs Peterson took both her wrists and manoeuvred them so that Judy was left standing bolt upright with her hands clasped across the top of her head as though she had just been taken prisoner. The position, which she remembered from her early days of running when she had quite frequently become out of breath, had the effect of taking some of the pressure off her ribs and allowed her to breathe much more deeply. It also had the unintended effect of leaving her feeling helplessly exposed, which would never have occurred to her before.

"That's better; good girl," said Mrs Peterson. "No, no, keep your hands above your—" Judy had thrown her arms down and sat herself among the roots of the tree. "Really, Judy, it was only lines. I don't understand why you are making such a fuss about this."

"It's the straw that broke the camel's back," she said, or tried to say, but she had lost her ability to enunciate.

Mrs Peterson sighed and dropped to her knees next to Judy. "Let's not worry about completing the run today, shall we? You'd better come home with me."

Judy felt hopelessly torn as Mrs Peterson chivvied her to her feet and marched her to the cottage. She was so very desperate for readmittance to that hallowed world of domestic comfort, but Mr Peterson had probably not left the house for morning roll call yet, and she could not bear to face him with her knuckles still smarting. "I'll be all right," said Judy weakly. "I'll go back to my dormitory and put my head down for a few minutes."

"Don't be silly. You just come with me."

Judy did not have the energy to fight with her and let herself be led in the direction of the cottage in an agony of uncertainty. "I can't," she said when they reached the gate. "Please!"

Mr Peterson was standing in the doorway watching them both calmly, and Judy knew with absolute certainty that the whole situation had been carefully planned. "Good morning, Judy," he said warmly. "You'd better come in."

Judy was almost more rattled by his kindness than she had been by his anger, and she avoided looking at him as Mrs Peterson marched her past him into the safety of the kitchen. She could see a boiled egg in its pale blue cup at Mr Peterson's place at the table, accompanied by a piece of buttered toast. "Sit down and let me get you a glass of water,"

78

said Mrs Peterson. She looked over her shoulder. "She's had a funny turn, nothing to worry about. Been overdoing it, I'll warrant."

Judy sat down heavily, as far from Mr Peterson's empty chair as possible, like a biblical guest taking the lowliest place to avoid being humiliated by the host. "I shall miss breakfast again," she said halfheartedly, for she had no particular desire to return to the refectory and lumpy porridge, apart from the desire to stay out of trouble for a few hours.

"You'll have breakfast with us this morning, Judy," announced Mrs Peterson in the matter-of-fact tone with which Judy had become familiar over the years. "I shall vouch for you if there's any trouble with Miss Miller. I'll say you were taken ill, which is scarcely a lie."

"There will be trouble," Judy almost whimpered. "If not the missed breakfast, I shall do *something* before the bell for morning break rings." Judy stared down at the table until she noticed Mr Peterson's hands resting on the surface directly opposite her. She did not lift her head. "I'm sorry about the other day, sir. I should never have used that word."

"Don't worry, Judy," he said at once. "No need to speak of it again; you've paid your penalty. Try to forget about it."

"There was no penalty for calling me a dirty little Jew, was there?" Judy retorted, glancing up at him for the first time. " 'Whore' is less insulting than 'dirty Jew'. One can choose to be a whore; one cannot choose to be a Jew."

"Judy, if you cannot accept an offer of forgiveness with good grace, it might be best to say nothing," answered Mr Peterson, sounding more disappointed than angry. "I demand that you let that matter drop. I've told you a thousand times, it's not healthy to bear a grudge."

79

Judy let her head drop onto her folded hands, crushed by the weight of a well-deserved rebuke. "Sorry," she mumbled, almost inaudibly. "I don't know why you don't expel me and have done with it."

"Because I'm not heartless enough to send you home to an angry father."

Judy heard the scrape of a plate being pushed in the direction of her head and sat up to find the boiled egg and toast being presented to her like a libation to calm a storm. "It's yours, sir."

"Ruby and her sister were considerate enough to lay two eggs early this morning. I shall have the other for breakfast tomorrow." He smiled at her indecision. She was properly enough brought up to know she should demur, but she was also hungry and eggs were becoming a rarity. "You tuck in."

Judy picked up the teaspoon guiltily and tapped her way around the top of the egg, breaking it open to reveal a perfect, soft-boiled yolk. She ate greedily without further encouragement, cutting the toast into soldiers and dipping them into the yolk the way she had done as a child. The Petersons settled themselves at the table, watching her eat. "Where's Annie?" she asked, between mouthfuls. She needed the reassurance of her long-lost friend with two concerned grown-ups watching her so intently.

Mr Peterson seemed to notice Annie's absence for the first time and glanced at his wife for an explanation. "She had to pop into school early," said Mrs Peterson gently. "Some prep she'd forgotten to finish last night. Don't worry, she's asked about you ever such a lot."

"I don't think she wants to be my friend now. Not that it matters—I never see anyone anymore," said Judy, but she was too distracted by the food to say anything further and filled her mouth in a most unladylike manner.

"You've had a rough few weeks, haven't you?" said Mr Peterson, taking advantage of her inability to answer. "You look tired."

Judy swallowed forcefully. "I have had a simply dreadful time, sir," she answered passionately. The offer of food had broken the ice between them. She was behaving every bit as he remembered. "Look at the state of my hands! And I must have written a million lines."

"I very much doubt it."

"And I have ever so much maths to do."

The Petersons exchanged glances. "Yes, I'd noticed you in the library every evening," said Mr Peterson. "What's that all about?" The question was mistimed; Judy had just crammed another mouthful of egg and toast into her mouth. "Are you in trouble with Mr Forbes as well? He hadn't mentioned anything to me."

Judy shook her head to buy herself some time before answering. "No, not at all. But he wants me to sit this very difficult exam, and he's making me do heaps of extra mathematics to prepare for it. He said the exam is mostly sat by much older people, even people who have been to university, but he believes I can pass it."

Mr Peterson rose to his feet and stepped away from the table to avoid the aroma of the breakfast he had sacrificed. "I wonder if this is all getting a little out of hand," he mused, looking back at Judy's bowed head. "Judy, if I have a word with Mr Forbes and ask him to give you less work to do, do you promise to make more of an effort to stay out of trouble?"

Judy looked positively hurt by the suggestion. "Sir, I have done nothing to get myself into trouble, I swear!"

"Judy—"

"Honestly, sir, I am quite sure I have been no naughtier this term than the last, but scarcely a day goes by when I'm not up to my neck in it! I know Miss Miller's behind all this; she doesn't want me to find out—"

"Judy, for the last time!"

"She's a Nazi! You know she is!"

The room descended into shocked silence, the word clattering about them like a glass being smashed against a tiled floor in slow motion. "That's quite an accusation, Judy," said Mr Peterson quietly. "I'd take that back if I were you."

Judy returned his glare with a cold glance of her own. "Would you prefer me to say 'traitor'?" she answered, too quickly to give herself the chance to reconsider. If the first word had been a breaking glass, the effect this time was more akin to a grenade being thrown into a corner of the room. The Petersons both winced visibly, waiting for the invisible dust to settle before either of them could consider an answer.

"Judy, please stop this at once," said Mrs Peterson, sitting beside her with a look of what was almost panic on her face. "This is wrong! It's true that Miss Miller dislikes you, and I am sorry if she is being unduly harsh, but—"

"She hates Jews," said Judy lamely, but she had crossed a line, and knew it. "You know she does."

"Yes, I know," she agreed, placing a hand on Judy's clenched fists, "and it is very wrong of her. But you cannot go about making accusations like this. Accusing a person of being a Nazi traitor is an extremely serious matter."

"Especially now," Mr Peterson put in. "As though there is not enough fear at the moment without encouraging that sort of hysteria. Now listen to me."

"Sir—" Judy made to stand up, but Mrs Peterson signalled for her to remain where she was, and she could not bring herself to resist. "I shall be late."

"You've eaten my breakfast; now you can spare me the time to listen," said Mr Peterson. A bell rang in the distance, tolling her impending doom. "You can make a dash for it now and you will be late for roll call, for which you will be punished, or you can wait five minutes and go into school with the two of us, who will vouch for you as we promised we would. It is entirely up to you."

Judy shook her head in miserable resignation, beaten by the bell, the empty eggshell and Mr Peterson's relentless logic. "I'm listening," she said.

"Good," he said, with only the slightest touch of sarcasm. "Now, listen carefully, because I have no intention of having this conversation with you again. Do you understand?" She nodded wearily. "You are to leave Miss Miller alone. I will not allow you to embark upon some ridiculous schoolgirl vendetta against a hated teacher that will only get you into trouble. Stay well out of her way. Do you understand?" Again, Judy nodded, more slowly this time. "I will never catch you using the word 'traitor' under any circumstances, or 'Nazi' unless you are speaking of Adolf Hitler himself."

"Sir—"

"Judy!"

"Yes, I understand."

"Treason in time of war is a very serious matter, Judy," warned Mr Peterson. "Traitors do not go to prison—they

83

hang, assuming they are not lynched before the authorities can kill them. It is not a term to be thrown around."

"I understand."

"Good girl. Now, I have some more pleasant news to share with you before Miss Miller announces it in assembly this morning. If we hurry, you'll have time to dash to your dormitory and change. I'll tell you on the way."

Judy drew a long breath as the Petersons got up and stepped into the vestibule to don hats and summer jackets. She had got through an entire conversation with a member of the older generation without being physically assaulted, handed out lines or ejected from the room. God could be thanked for the smallest of mercies.

7

In years to come, there would be few moments of that term that Judy would remember with any great fondness: the exhilaration of crossing the finishing line first, a giddy half hour with a friend, a moment of unexpected hilarity after lights-out—fragments of calm before the storm overwhelmed them, so difficult to recall above the swirling mists of her worst memory. But the mind is cruel in its determination to remember the pain, the terror, the misery of past years so much more vividly than an innocent joy. And there were innocent joys, even in that most fateful of terms; there were days during those precious few weeks after Miss Miller's announcement when Judy wished to be nowhere else.

The announcement, delivered by Miss Miller in such a terse, dispassionate manner that the sleepier members of the school might easily have missed it altogether, was that the school was to participate in the "Dig for Victory" campaign. Miss Miller was gracious enough to acknowledge to the school that the plan had been devised by Mr Forbes, who believed that the school should be making the most of its extensive grounds to provide as much of its own food as possible, and she had decided to give the project her blessing. Without wishing to turn the school into a farm, Miss Miller would permit large swaths of the gardens and scrubland to be ploughed for crops, as long as the playing fields were not touched.

Judy had already found out from Mr Forbes that he had grown up on a farm. On long summer evenings, when Judy found herself working her way through ever more fiendishly difficult calculations whilst her friends played cricket on the lawns outside, she would endeavour to distract Mr Forbes by feigning interest in his life. Distracting the teacher was the oldest trick in the book of naughty pupils, and Mr Forbes was sensible enough to focus his attention squarely on simultaneous equations in the classroom, valiantly fending off any attempt to draw him on another subject. In the more relaxed setting of a one-to-one lesson, however, Judy found it a great deal easier to catch Mr Forbes off guard, and their many digressions together made his long encroachments into her free time almost bearable.

It gave her the chance to clear the air about a subject that had stubbornly refused to dislodge itself from her mind, as her mistakes so seldom did. "I'm awfully sorry I asked why you were not a soldier," she said, ten minutes into a session. Mr Forbes had set her a mock exam paper to try out and was sitting in the opposite corner of the deserted library with some marking. "It was remiss of me."

Mr Forbes looked up at her with a vacant look Judy found strangely endearing. "Judy, that was weeks ago. You oughtn't to let things prey on your mind. I'd forgotten all about it."

"I'm afraid things do rather," confessed Judy, chewing the end of her pencil as though she seriously intended to get on with the task at hand. "I felt awful about it when I realised you'd had polio. I thought you were a conscientious objector at first. I'd hate you to think I thought you were a conchy."

"It wasn't polio, as a matter of fact," answered Mr Forbes,

86

putting down his red pen. Judy took it as a sign that he was conceding the battle before he could lose it, and let her pencil fall from her fingers. "It's an affliction from birth."

"Oh. I'm sorry." Judy was startled by an unexpected feeling of sympathy for him, accompanied by the same sense of embarrassment she had felt when she had first noticed his limp on the train. She gave up on the conversation and busied herself with her work, muttering, "How awful, I'm sorry" rather stupidly as she lowered her eyes.

"No need to be sorry; I shan't be needing your pity," he said to her bowed head. "My father taught me not to be troubled by it. He always treated me like my brothers and expected me to get on with things."

Judy looked up again cautiously, blushing as she caught his eye. She did not find eye contact at all easy for all her outward confidence, and she was unsettled by the connection it seemed to make between them. "Wasn't it . . ." She struggled to say the words. "Wasn't it difficult living on a farm? I mean, difficult when your brothers were all dashing about?"

"Not at all," he assured her. "I was the youngest. The older ones carried me about. Then my father taught me to ride. My lame leg didn't hold me back then."

Judy's eyes widened with the thought. She was a townie in every sense of the word, brought up among the brick-and-stone jungle of the capital. Unlike some of the other girls, she had never been anywhere near a horse before, and she breathed in sharply just imagining herself going anywhere near such a powerful animal. "Gosh," she managed to say. "I've never been on a horse. My father thought it might be dangerous."

Mr Forbes got up and moved over to Judy, sitting down

at the table opposite her. The table where Judy was working was too narrow for two people working opposite one another, and he felt a little too close to her, but she made no attempt at drawing back as he leaned forward to talk to her. "You've never lived," he whispered, as though sharing a secret he had never spoken to anyone. "It's the most extraordinary feeling in the world, Judy. Galloping across the fields with the sun on one's back. No one could catch me then."

Judy imagined him riding gallantly across an open field, his white shirt billowing like a sail in the early morning breeze. She dropped her head down again, closing her eyes to hide her embarrassment. "Sir, why are you making me do all this?" she asked, desperately clawing her way to the safety of the mathematics paper. "You still haven't told me what this test is all about. Is it something to do with Oxford? My father said he would quite like me to go to Oxford, but I thought perhaps—"

"No, it's not the Oxford entrance exam I am preparing you for," said Mr Forbes, as though to reassure her. "I've told you, this is a different test, something very important. I'm afraid I can't tell you a lot about it at the moment, only that you should work very hard to pass it."

Judy sat back in her chair. "But when am I to take the test? And where? Shall I have to travel to London?"

"You'll take the test when I am satisfied that you are ready to take it," he said, which only made everything sound a good deal more mysterious than he evidently meant it to, "and you'll take it here. The paper will be sent to me, and you will do the test in isolation, probably in Miss Miller's office, with a teacher watching over you to make sure you can't cheat."

"You?"

"No, or I might be tempted to help you." Mr Forbes picked up her pencil and pressed it into her hand. "Come on now, you're wasting time."

Thirty seconds later, Judy was hunched over her work again, and Mr Forbes was back in his place across the room, sabotaging a pile of copybooks with explosions of indignant red ink.

~

Everything felt very different in the open air, with a whole team of girls attacking the lawns with spades. Mr Forbes had worked out the plans for cultivating vegetables with military precision. There were to be ten vegetable patches to begin with, connected by grass walkways (the strips of lawn they were instructed not to dig up) wide enough to walk two abreast to avoid accidents. The vast squares of ground to be dug up were measured out by the gardener, who marked out the four corners by hammering small wooden stakes into the ground and winding twine right the way round. The girls were divided into teams of five per plot and were instructed to work steadily and systematically to clear the grass.

Crops were planned according to the time of year and which vegetables were deemed to be the most filling and nutritious. Two plots were set aside for potatoes, followed by carrots, onions, cabbages, peas, beetroot, marrow, swedes and turnips. The Petersons were handed the task of purchasing and building homes for chickens (they were regarded as experts in this area on account of their own pet chickens), which they duly did with the help of the more dexterous older girls who could be trusted with hammers and saws. Mr Forbes asked Annie and Judy to act as egg collectors for the much-anticipated basketfuls of breakfast the chickens were sure to provide, while others took on the tasks of feeding and cleaning; Mr Forbes silently decided that he would be the one to wring the necks of any unproductive chickens when none of the girls was looking.

"If I didn't know better, I'd say everyone is in a better mood since we started all this," Judy mused to Annie, as they knelt side by side planting carrot seeds. "I have managed a whole three days without getting into trouble."

"Perhaps you're in a better mood," teased Annie, sitting back on her heels. "Not as much time on your hands playing at being a spy."

Judy frowned, trying hard to take the comment in good part. *I'm not playing at anything!* She would quite like to have said but did not have the energy for an argument. *I know she's a Nazi! I know she is! I simply have to prove it!* "Well, this lot is certainly keeping me busy. It would have to have been our patch that he made a fuss about clearing. Every single teeny-weeny little stone!"

"It's not a penance, I promise," said a rumbling voice behind them, making the girls jump. Mr Forbes had predictably appeared behind them to inspect their progress, just in time to hear them moaning. "Carrot patches are always a pig to clear. You'll get some very interesting-looking carrots if you don't, and you probably won't want to eat them when they've split five ways."

"I think they'd look beautiful!" squeaked Annie. "Imagine eating a star-shaped carrot for lunch."

Miss Miller had also come out to inspect the girls' progress, or rather to ensure that none of them was enjoying herself too much, and her birdlike figure could be seen striding across the walkway at the other side of the patch. Mr Forbes, as affable as ever, waved in her direction. "Miss Miller, come and look at what the girls have been up to! We'll have mountains of food to harvest in time for the new term."

Miss Miller stopped in her tracks and turned to acknowledge Mr Forbes and the girls glancing expectantly in her direction. Judy was keen to see if Miss Miller was churlish enough to answer Mr Forbes' friendly greeting with her usual sour response. Setting aside her personal beliefs about Miss Miller's political sympathies, Judy felt a peculiar fascination regarding her headmistress, much the way a small rodent might be intrigued by a snake, moments before being eaten alive. The old woman (since everyone over the age of thirty was tragically ancient) regarded them with her customarily cold displeasure. Miss Miller could not have known it—nor would she have greatly cared—but she was Judy's own personal vision of hell, down to the taut contours of her permanently clenched teeth and the lines around her eyes and mouth, delineating her every scowl and sneer for the past thirty-five years. Through Judy's eyes, she was a menacing warning of what might happen to her if she took too many wrong turns in life and failed to achieve her dreams. She too might become a hell-bound harpy kept on this earth to torment the living: *all the wicked spirits who wander the earth seeking the ruin of souls.*

"Splendid!" declared Miss Miller with a professional smile that reeked of insincerity. "And who, pray, will care for these vast vegetable patches when the girls have all returned home? Or were you thinking of incarcerating them here all summer?"

Mr Forbes pretended not to notice her sneering tone. "Not to worry, Miss Miller, I've got it all worked out. Haven't I, girls?" He winked conspiratorially at Annie and Judy, but the attempt at camaraderie seemed only to rile Miss Miller, who picked her way along the pathway in their direction.

"I sincerely hope you do have it all worked out, Mr Forbes," she answered, with enforced cheerfulness that still managed to sound threatening. "I doubt the school will take kindly to returning to piles of moulding turnips at the beginning of the new school year." Miss Miller glanced disdainfully at Judy's filthy fingernails. "Well done, dear," she added before making to walk away. "You'll make a superb labourer's wife one day."

Judy flinched at the insult, but before she could make an angry retort, she felt Mr Forbes' boot hitting her ankle, causing her to fall to her knees. He immediately stooped down to help her to her feet, hushing her indignant cry with "Upsy-daisy, mind how you go now!"

"I didn't f—"

"Easy does it. The ground's quite slippery after last night's rain."

Judy took the hint with the utmost reluctance and waited until Miss Miller was out of earshot before turning on him. "What did you do that for?" she demanded, nursing her ankle, which was not hurting especially, but she wanted to make him feel as guilty as possible. "You kicked me!"

"I did no such thing; I simply threw you off balance," he said, stifling laughter, but Annie was already in stitches, and

Judy could not for the life of her see the joke. "You would only have said something appalling and given her reason to hurt you, you numpty! I thought I'd spare you the humiliation."

"I don't care. You should have let me say something. I'll be fit to explode all day now!"

"You might have cared a little by the time you found yourself in her study," Mr Forbes chuckled, extending a hand to make peace with her. Judy folded her arms. "Come on, Judy, you're always complaining that you're never out of trouble. You should thank me."

Judy squeaked with indignation, an unfortunate mannerism that made her sound like a guinea pig and provoked more laughter from Annie and Mr Forbes. "*Thank* you? Are you mad?" Impulsively, she gave Mr Forbes a light shove, aware that she was breaking some unspoken rule somewhere, but he responded as she had expected, with more laughter and a look of mock hurt.

"Is that any way to treat a lame schoolmaster?" he asked, pushing her in return, but Judy darted out of the way, colliding with Annie. A second later, the madness of the moment had caught up with the girls farther along the line, and the seed planting was abandoned in favour of a game of impromptu tag, which Mr Forbes made no attempt to stop. His own childhood had been punctuated by giddy episodes like this, when youth had taken over and children had been permitted the anarchic grace of childhood, but he hoped no one would note his willingness to let discipline break down around him.

From a discreet distance, Mr Peterson watched his young friend's lapse in judgement as the girls in his care—including

Peterson's own daughter—tumbled about in a manner that would be deemed unseemly even in the playground. Forbes was a useful brother-at-arms in a school where fault lines were invisibly appearing all over the place, but he was a young man in the wrong place, which made him dangerous and perhaps in danger without knowing it. Peterson would have to talk to him before Miss Miller became suspicious of him or he did something indiscreet. Another wild card to rein in, thought Peterson, turning his back and walking the long way round to the school to avoid being forced to intervene. And a grown man was infinitely more difficult to control. Not that any of this could go on much longer. Peterson doubted that there would be anyone left—even his family—to harvest those vegetables when the time came, but he was the only one who could see it.

8

"I couldn't help thinking that Annie looked like exactly the sort of girl who *would* be made a form captain," admitted Mr Peterson, as he stepped into the cottage with Mary. Lessons ended at lunchtime on a Saturday, and he had promised to take Annie fishing as a reward for her elevation to the inner sanctum of prefects. "Standing on the stage as pleased as punch with an approving headmistress pinning a badge to her lapel. She might have been an illustration for an Angela Brazil story."

Mary sat on the stairs and unlaced her shoes. The fatigue of middle age always hit her at that point in the week after many hours of dashing about, calling out commands to reluctant cricket players and maintaining her enthusiasm whilst exposed to every possible weather pattern an English summer could throw at her. "You must be sure to make a fuss of her; she's not having an easy term."

Peterson hung up his coat. "Do you think not? I hadn't noticed anything amiss."

"That's because you're a man," said Mary cheerfully, handing him her shoes. He obligingly took them from her and placed them near the door. "It's all right; it's just Judy being absent so much. She's missing her, that's all."

"I'd noticed she's been a bit quiet," Peterson said, though in truth he had been far too preoccupied with his own concerns to notice that his daughter was being a little reclusive. "Should I invite Judy to join us on the fishing trip?"

Mary raised an eyebrow. "Darling, I should very much like to have a few little beauties to cook tonight if it's all the same to you. Poor Judy's such a fidget, she'll only end up falling in or something and scaring away all the fish." The corners of Mary's mouth flickered. "Well, actually, in her current frame of mind, she'll probably get into a blazing row with the fish."

Peterson laughed. "Poor thing, she does mean frightfully well. I could ask her to mind the bait or something, well away from the water's edge."

Mary walked into the kitchen, letting her husband place a hand around her waist as she passed him. "She won't be able to go anyway; she's confined to her dormitory until suppertime. Fell foul of—"

"Here we go again. Is Annie eating here or in the refectory?" asked Peterson, more sharply than he had intended. "I'm ravenous."

"Why don't you set the table for the two of us?" suggested Mary, removing half a loaf from the bread bin, "and put out the pot of beef dripping in the larder. I think she said she'd eat in the ref with Judy to cheer her up. I'm afraid I rather encouraged her to eat over there. The food stretches further that way."

Peterson watched as Mary cut the loaf as thin as she could; he felt a knot of anxiety tightening in his chest. "Don't worry, darling, we'll come back with a couple of fat trout for supper." He stepped into the larder in search of the pot and stared at the shelves with their neat and tidy tins and jars standing in order of height. *But when she got there, the cupboard was bare, and so the poor doggy had none.* "It's good of Annie to keep Judy company," he said, for the sake of maintaining the conversation. There it was, the lid covered in a square of cloth with an embroidered cow across the top. "Anything else, darling?"

"There might be a few gherkins left," said Mary.

The cupboard was hardly bare, thought Peterson, closing the door slowly. It was the absence of colour he was noticing, the empty spaces where a nice juicy ham would have hung once or a bright yellow bunch of bananas. He wondered whether Annie's absences were really based upon a desire to spend time with Judy—though he had no reason to doubt it—or whether she was trying not to put too much of a strain on the family's resources. "You know, she needn't martyr herself in the school refectory," Peterson remarked. "We're not starving. Yet."

Mary turned from the breadboard in exasperation. "Nobody's going to starve!" she exclaimed. "You're always saying that! Food is short. That's not the same thing."

"Mary, put the knife down!" he pleaded, raising his hands in mock surrender. "It's not that bad!"

Mary looked down at her own hand and realised she had been waving the breadknife in her husband's face, having forgotten to put it down before she turned to remonstrate with him. She placed it gingerly on the breadboard, laughing with the effort. "At least we won't get fat in our old age."

They stood in silence in one another's arms, enjoying a few minutes of rare calm in a busy world of timetables and noisy girls. The marbled blue sky on the other side of the window promised a balmy afternoon out on the river, but for a moment, Peterson stroked his wife's silver-dusted head. They would grow old together. He wanted to believe that more than anything. They would sit together in years to come, when the war was a reassuringly distant memory, enjoying the privilege of old age that so many were denied. They would play with their grandchildren. With his wife leaning peacefully against him, Peterson could believe that any number of miracles might be possible.

~

There was something idiosyncratically English about standing up to the waist in freezing cold water for hours at a time, awaiting the joyous sensation of dinner tugging on the end of the line. And doing it voluntarily. Choosing to spend a sunny afternoon staring down at the swirling waters and rippling duckweed, pondering the weightier questions of human existence. Peterson always felt at peace here; there were no ghosts in the river to leap out at him when he least expected it, and the waterways had not been entangled in barbed wire to keep Jerry out.

"It was ever so sporting of you to come fishing with your old man," said Peterson gratefully, smiling at the ludicrous sight of Annie standing a short distance from him in the water. Annie was the sort of girl who always looked a little ungainly, slightly too tall to be elegant and still in the habit of hunching her shoulders when she felt self-conscious. She reminded her father unhelpfully of a stork, perched awkwardly on long, thin legs with her hair scraped back in a feathery blonde crown. "You're doing very well."

Annie grinned. "First time I've ever caught one on my

own," she said proudly, "though I do wish the fish wouldn't struggle so terribly when one drags them out of the water. It's horrid."

Peterson shrugged. "It's in the nature of living things to struggle," he said, then swiftly changed the subject. It was just like a young mind to notice something macabre in an otherwise innocent scene. "I meant being made a form captain. I'm very proud of you."

"I want to make you proud of me," she said, blushing at the unexpected compliment. "It's nice to come first for a change."

Peterson glanced over at her in surprise. It was unlike her to be bitter, but he could not miss the resentful tone. "There's more to life than winning, Annie; I promise. But you should feel very proud to be trusted by Miss Miller. She knows you are worthy of the responsibility." He hesitated, noting that Annie had already resumed her cheerful demeanour for him. "You must be getting hungry," he ventured. "Why don't we take a little break? We've got a good catch."

Annie took the hint and came squelching and staggering towards him, laughing with the effort of moving through the sticky, slimy mud. "I thought you'd never ask!" she sighed. "Did you bring us anything to eat?"

Peterson reached a hand out to her, but she made her way to the riverbank without incident and settled herself near a patch of long grass, her booted feet still dangling in the water. "I think your mother packed some sandwiches. They're in my knapsack." He hauled himself out of the water, packing away the fishing tackle whilst Annie searched for the promised refreshments. He suspected that they would not be returning to the water; they had managed to coax three tasty-looking specimens onto their lines. They could return to the cottage in triumph.

"Save some for me, won't you?" He settled himself next to Annie, waiting patiently as she opened the thermos and poured tea into two enamel mugs. "Just the ticket."

This was happiness, he thought: sitting on the riverbank sharing tasteless cheese sandwiches and tepid tea with his daughter. A noisy gaggle of ducks swam past in untidy formation, disturbing the silence. Peterson watched as Annie leaned forward and scattered crumbs onto the water to coax them towards her. "You weren't hoping for roast duck as well tonight, were you?" enquired Peterson.

"Oh, Dad, that's beastly!" squealed Annie, causing the ducks to remove themselves from her vicinity without taking up the offer of bread. "The poor things!"

"You're right—it wouldn't taste right without a few slices of orange," Peterson conceded. "Is there any more tea?"

Annie handed him the thermos. "If the Germans invade, will they come here?"

"Not unless they want to benefit from a good solid education," answered Peterson wryly. "Brush up those Latin declensions. What's Judy been telling you this time?"

Annie shook her head. The need to protect her errant friend was practically reflexive these days. "Nothing. Everyone's talking about it."

"Everyone?"

Annie could never hold out long under her father's inquisitorial gaze and flushed with embarrassment. "Well, she knows so much more than everyone else! I don't know where she finds out about it all. I can never keep up with what she's saying. I always feel so stupid!"

Peterson moved a little closer to Annie and put his arm around her. "You know, you mustn't worry about all of this; it's not your concern. It's not Judy's concern either." She made no answer, but Peterson knew he was responding to entirely the wrong point. "Annie, you mustn't compare yourself with Judy; you've never done so before. You're very different girls, and that's all to the good. It's why you've always been such friends."

Annie nodded vigorously, indicating that she was not convinced at all. "Oh, I know. I don't mind one bit," she ventured. She was the sort of girl who knew precisely what was expected of her and was normally quite good at meeting the expectation. "Truly I don't. But I suppose I shouldn't mind being a little better at maths . . ."

"Your atrocious algebra we can do something about," promised Peterson with a smile, "but you wouldn't want to be like Judy, I promise. It's hard to be different, and she is different."

Annie picked at the crust of her sandwich. "I suppose I can't help thinking it must be more interesting somehow."

"It's not at all interesting for the person; it's just hard," said Peterson firmly, noting Annie's fidgeting fingers. "It is never easy to stand out from the crowd. Being gifted is a small consolation, even if it doesn't seem that way to you. And it is very, very hard to grow up without a mother. You've no idea, thank God."

"I'm sorry."

There was a long, painful conversation waiting to be had, but for all his fluency in multiple languages, Peterson had never found the words to tell the story that mattered to him the most. He stood up, shaking the crumbs off his clothing. "Nothing to be sorry about. One recovers, but I think I know something of what Judy must have felt, watching her mother take ill and die." He glanced down at Annie, who had stuffed the remaining food in her mouth, more to obviate the need to answer than to satisfy hunger. He knew she was desperate for him to stop. "We should probably get back while the fish are still nice and fresh," he said, offering Annie a hand getting up. She appeared not to notice and turned over onto her front to push herself onto her feet. The waders posed more of a problem than she had anticipated, restricting the movement of her knees."Annie, I wouldn't—"

"I can manage," she said, but her foot, still partly in the water, snagged on a clump of duckweed, and she began to slide down the soft, loamy bank. "Help!"

Peterson knew he would never reach her without falling flat on his face, and he was laughing too much to try. He watched as his daughter scrabbled helplessly for something to hold on to, the heavy rubber waders pulling her farther and farther down until she gave up altogether and fell into the river with an ignominious splash. He stepped effortlessly back into the water and fished her out by the waist, hoping his wife would see the funny side when he arrived back at the cottage with three splendid fish and a soaking-wet daughter covered in mud and slime. "Don't worry, you'll be nice and dry by the time we get home," promised Peterson, with the tone of a matron telling a child that being stabbed in the arm with a hypodermic needle "won't hurt a bit".

Annie attempted a good-natured laugh as she slipped her hand into her pocket in search of her handkerchief. Fortunately for Annie, she had her mother's cool head and was quite well disposed towards wildlife of all kinds, as there was something soft and smooth wriggling under her fingers. "I was hot anyway," said Annie, beaming as she very carefully secured the frog in her hand before it could hop out of her pocket. "Could you give me a hand getting out in case I fall again?"

"Of course," said Peterson, reaching out to her without looking; he was trying to work out how much longer it was going to take them to walk home with Annie staggering about in wet clothes. He noted the sudden presence of an imposter in the palm of his hand a second before the frog jumped in his face, hitting him neatly between the eyes before hopping into his hair and jumping clear. Unfortunately, he was really quite squeamish about amphibians and let out an unmanly shriek, staggering back so violently to remove the creature from his hair that he lost his footing and fell backwards, flailing desperately as he disappeared up to his neck in the water.

"Don't worry, you'll be nice and dry by the time we get home," promised Annie, offering a helping hand.

"Don't bother!" spluttered Peterson. "There's probably a snake up your sleeve!"

They walked home across the fields, Annie feeling a good deal better about her tumble than she had expected, Peterson trying to work out how best to get them both undercover before one of his fellow teachers—or, horror of horrors, one of his pupils—spotted them. "I've never heard you scream like that, Dad," said Annie, which was the wrong comment at the wrong moment, but Peterson made a calculated decision to be heartily amused by the whole business.

"We all have our little nightmares, darling," he said. "Mine happens to be small, cold, wriggly things." Yes, that much was true. He loathed frogs. But he could not recall a single one of his many nightmares involving them. "One should remain open-minded about such things. One man's meat is another man's poison. My nightmare is the Frenchman's delicious meal."

"You're not cross, are you?"

"Certainly not. I shan't even make you gut the fish to make up for it."

Peterson thought of the family dinner once they had bathed and changed and smelled a little more tolerable. He might suggest that they play the gramophone as they ate instead of listening to the wireless with its sudden, unpredictable announcements. He might even read aloud to them the way he had done when the children were younger. In his mind, he constructed layers and layers of invisible battlements around his family home, sealing off the vulnerable points of entry, stocking up on provisions, pulling up the drawbridge. All was well.

9

Mr Forbes had many bright ideas that term in his enthusiasm to prove his worth at a new school, but the idea of buying a Spitfire to blast the Luftwaffe out of the sky was mercifully not his. According to Annie, who—by virtue of being the daughter of two teachers—knew all the gossip from the inner sanctum of the staff room, the idea originated with Miss Geoffry, the history teacher. The town where she had grown up had clubbed together and held large numbers of jumble sales and the like to raise funds. As a reward for their efforts, somewhere circling the airy blue there was a Spitfire with *West Laverton* painted proudly on one wing. If West Laverton could contribute to the defence of the realm, Mulwith School could do the same.

"There was a frightful row about it, apparently," said Annie for good measure. Annie was not so underendowed in the brains department to have failed to notice her reputation as the nice-but-none-too-bright girl of the class, better suited to a cricket field than a classroom any day. There were, however, a few precious occasions like this when she knew something Judy did not, and she relished every single word they exchanged over cups of lukewarm tea. "Miss Miller wanted nothing to do with such a harebrained scheme."

"That's interesting," mused Judy, reaching for the teapot then remembering herself. She was still scared to death of touching the Peterson family's china, having once managed to break the teapot they had been given as a wedding present. It had been one of her early visits to the house, just to make the situation as excruciatingly embarrassing as possible, and she had offered to make the tea in an attempt at making herself useful. She still could not remember how she had come to slip on the kitchen floor shortly after filling the pot, but in her panic, she had grabbed wildly for something to hold on to and caught hold of the teapot. It had smashed on the edge of the cupboard as she dragged it towards her, a stream of boiling tea and broken fragments of china fell all around her, narrowly missing her as she fell in an inglorious heap on the floor. The incident was still a family joke, as was the need for someone else to fill Judy's cup for her.

"Don't overegg the pudding," came a calm bass voice from the doorway. Mr Peterson had entered, ostensibly to look for tea, but Judy suspected he had been eavesdropping from the hall for a while. "There was no such thing; there was a frank exchange of views. I assure you, no china was smashed in the process."

He gave Judy a wink as he reached for the teapot, causing her to redden predictably before letting out a giggle. "You do look awfully funny like that, sir," she said, holding out her cup hopefully. He paid back her irreverence by walking away with the teapot, which looked quite absurd in his hand, covered in a bright pink tea cosy gathered at the top with pink and blue pom-poms. He picked up a cup and saucer from the cupboard and proceeded to pour himself the rest of the tea, noting with evident annoyance that the girls had drunk most of the milk.

"I know precisely what is going on in your suspicious

little mind, Judy," he continued, stirring the dregs of the milk into the dregs of the tea; the combination would be ghastly, but drinking tea was an unbreakable habit, however it tasted. "For your information, Miss Miller is understandably a little concerned at the prospect of raising a large sum of money to buy an object that will be used to end lives."

"Or to save them, I suppose," Judy put in, "according to the catechism . . ."

"Yes, well, whether a weapon may be described as offensive or defensive rather depends upon which side of the gun one is standing on," answered Mr Peterson glibly, sitting down next to Annie, "and I'm not sure Miss Miller is especially interested in the Church's teachings."

Judy gave a satisfied smile. "I told you, fifth columnist."

"Define fifth columnist, Judy," answered Mr Peterson, tonelessly, "if you can."

Judy faltered. "If she doesn't believe the country should be fighting the Germans—"

"She may well be a pacifist for all you know—there are a few of those—or she may simply disapprove of involving children in the war effort."

"Plenty of children will die. Perhaps she approves . . . sorry."

"I think that's enough," said Mr Peterson quietly, without looking up from his cup. "When you've both finished feeling pleased with yourselves, kindly remember that the rest of us have seen wars before, and that includes Miss Miller. Please forgive the old for not being quite enthusiastic enough for you."

～

When it came to it, Judy was not as enthusiastic as she might have been either, but not because of any pacifist or pro-German sentiments. It was all very well talking about assisting the war effort, but while men were joining the army and women were joining the Women's Auxiliary Air Force, Mulwith School's first attempt at Spitfire fundraising involved a week of intensive rehearsals for a concert to which the people of the nearby villages were invited. There were to be no ticket sales, but pairs of smiling girls with baskets were to stand at the doors at the end of the concert to collect donations.

Judy, who was one step away from tone deaf, was placed strategically at the back of the choir by the music mistress Mrs Ingrams and instructed to mime in time with the music. Some of this deceit was unnecessary, as Judy was far too short to stand at the back of the choir and was completely obscured by Beryl standing directly in front of her. Knowing that she was not permitted to offend the audience with her tuneless warbling, Judy was not sure why it was strictly necessary for her to attend every one of the tediously long rehearsals, especially when she knew all the songs backwards and forwards.

Only the writing of endless lines was a worse horror for Judy than music practice in that vast assembly hall with its splintered floorboards that smelled perpetually of fruity wood polish, and long windows framed by faded green curtains that had not been replaced since the death of the old queen. But then, Mrs Ingrams' piano had probably not had any tender loving care since that time either, the way it clanked and buzzed, always leaving a murmur of half-remembered chords hovering in the air after the teacher's hands had left the keys.

"Cheer up, Judy, it may never happen!" called out Mrs Ingrams with unbearable brightness as they took their places. Judy took advantage of her immediate disappearance from the teacher's sight to scowl at the back of the girl in front.

"It has happened; I'm here," answered Judy, causing the rest of the soprano section to burst into fits of giggles.

Mrs Ingrams, a widow from the Great War, had adopted a mask of cheeriness so many years ago that it had become permanently welded to her face. Judy—who could smell deceit a mile away—suspected that Mrs Ingrams was not of a naturally sunny disposition but that she could not remember now what her true character had been and why she had felt the need to hide it. "That's enough!" she responded, playing a four-octave arpeggio, which quickly settled the girls. "I can think of infinitely worse places to be, my girl. Now let's begin with something nice and rousing, shall we?"

> Bring me my bow of burning gold!
> Bring me my arrows of desire!

"Louder, girls! Sing it with feeling!" Mrs Ingrams called out above the chorus of unenthusiastic voices cutting through the dusty air. "Imagine the room bursting with people!"

> Bring me my spear! O clouds unfold!
> Bring me my chariot of fire!

Now there was a song to stir the heart, even Judy's, as she stood peering through the gap made by Beryl's and Lizzy's shoulders at the dust swirling around in the shafts of afternoon sunlight. She enjoyed the song even though it reminded her uncomfortably of the time during her early childhood when she had attempted to entertain her parents' dinner guests with a song and mistaken the words "chariot of fire" for "chariot on fire". She had wondered for an awfully long time afterwards why all the grown-ups had found her singing so hilarious.

In the event, credit had to be given to the team of girls, led by Annie, who had spent Saturday afternoon going door-to-door around the village, advertising the event. For a concert that had been pulled together at the last minute, there was a splendid turnout on the day, with most of the inhabitants of the village and local town present, along with some of the parents who lived within an easy journey. Judy endeavoured to count the rows of guests stretching back the length of the hall, but it was not an easy task, as the entire audience had stood up at the sound of Mrs Ingrams belting out the famous opening chords of "Jerusalem" on the piano.

Now I am truly not needed, thought Judy, her mouth opening and shutting dutifully to the words of the great hymn. It was surprisingly hard to mime a familiar hymn, to stifle the reflex to make noise (even an offensive noise, in Judy's case), when everyone in the vicinity is united in song; it left her feeling bored and unwelcome. Few people enjoy the sense of being surplus to requirements, and Judy was particularly testy on the subject. She might have risked skiving off the whole concert if she had thought she might get away with it, but the girls had a special concert dress they were obliged to wear for public performances, and Judy had known that if she did not turn up to get changed, someone would notice the lone navy blue frock with white ribbons that had not been claimed. She had also suspected that Miss Miller would take a head count as they filed in to ensure that no one had helped herself to an afternoon off. Never one to avoid an opportunity to tick boxes, Miss Miller had indeed stood at the back of the hall with her trusty clipboard and pencil, ticking off the girls' names as they filed slowly past her in single file. As the girls reached the stage and fanned out into three crescent-shaped rows, Miss Miller had discreetly taken up her place at the front, ready to welcome the concertgoers in simpering tones.

Once Miss Miller had been established in her place of honour, escape from her was impossible. Except that Miss Miller was no longer there. Judy could see quite clearly that Miss Miller was no longer in her seat and had almost certainly never returned after the short break. It was quite possible of course that she had been forced to step out to attend to some business or other, a telephone call perhaps, or one of those small, frequent emergencies that disrupt a headmistress' time.

She's gone to meet someone, thought Judy immediately. *She's using the concert as a smokescreen so that she can slip away to do something dastardly.* Judy had no concept of an innocent or trivial explanation at the best of times, but with her imagination running riot over a period of weeks, she could not resist the idea that Miss Miller was up to no good and that she was being given a perfect opportunity to find out the truth at long last.

Judy had only a moment to make a decision. Once the hymn had finished, the audience would sit down and the choir would begin the next song, making it harder for her to disappear unnoticed. Judy glanced to her right and realised that she was quite close to the edge of the stage curtain, meaning that if she ducked her head down slightly and took just two or three steps to the right, she would disappear from Mrs Ingrams' field of vision.

"What are you doing?" whispered Beatrice in her ear as Judy disappeared into the folds of the curtain. "You'll cop it!"

Judy raised a finger to her lips in desperation, noting that the entire back row was watching her slipping away. She would have to rely on schoolgirl honour to keep her safe this time, on the unwritten rule that you never split on anyone ever, even if she were your worst enemy. As Mrs Ingrams thundered her way through the final chords, Judy sneaked out of the hall through the narrow wooden back door, down the stone spiral staircase and out of the building via the boot room.

It was unexpectedly cool outside, and Judy shivered in her thin cotton dress. Worse, having given Mrs Ingrams the slip, Judy now had absolutely no idea what to do next. Miss Miller could be in all manner of places, in any part of the building or in any corner of the grounds; and since the concert would be over in just over an hour and Miss Miller would have to have returned by then, Judy had very little time to find out what the woman was up to.

As she dashed under the cover of the trees—an obvious place for a seasoned spy to hide—she sensed the odour of rough tobacco smoke in her nostrils and knew immediately that she had company. Male company of the pipe-smoking variety.

"I ought to turn you in right now," said Mr Forbes, taking Judy by the shoulder and wheeling her around to face him. "What are you up to this time?"

"Does Miss Miller know you've skived off the concert to have a smoke?" asked Judy by way of self-defence, a little more pertly than she had intended.

Forbes coloured with either anger or embarrassment. "I'd get back to the concert if I were you, unless you'd rather I frogmarched you back into the hall myself."

Judy went into conciliatory mode. "Please don't be cross. I'm . . . I'm looking for Miss Miller. She's left the concert, you see. I thought perhaps that something had happened . . ."

Forbes rolled his eyes. "Judy, you're really not cut out for this, are you? Your face is like a picture book."

"But she slipped out when she thought no one was looking!"

Forbes was suddenly deadly serious. "Judy, you really are incapable of listening to anyone, aren't you? I don't know what you think you're playing at, but you've got some absurd idea in your head, and you are going to get yourself into terrible trouble. If Miss Miller has left the concert, it is for a good reason, and it is absolutely none of your business. Now, you must go back inside."

Judy hesitated for a moment, glancing at her teacher's face for any sign that he might change his mind, but his look was resolute. She nodded miserably and scarpered out of sight, watching from a distance as he turned his back and walked away.

It was a ludicrous thing for him to tell her to do anyway, thought Judy, as she lay in wait for him to disappear. She could not possibly slip back into the concert now. It had been risky enough to leave, and someone would be sure to notice her reentrance. She would have to lie low until it was all over and try to find some way of getting back to the dressing room and changed before anyone noticed she had been absent. Unfortunately for Judy, she could never think through a plan carefully enough before she threw herself into it. Now that she considered matters, it was hard to see how she had ever imagined she could avoid Mrs Ingrams' finding out that she had slunk out of the concert. Judy had been too intent upon discovering Miss Miller, imagining that she would discover something so formidable that no one would care about her absence.

Well, thought Judy, as she made her way stealthily towards the coastal path, knowing that she would be well sheltered from prying eyes, the very worst that would happen was that she would have to admit to being bored and leaving the concert. She would be in trouble again: there would be detention, lines and the loss of a few privileges, but no one need know what she had been up to, and Mr Forbes would probably not split on her. She was getting quite good at making the best of a disastrous situation.

Based on the premise that she might as well hang for sheep as for lamb, Judy slipped out-of-bounds, disappearing into the tunnel of green gloom near which she had been so rudely accosted in the name of national security such a short time before. She suspected that the granddad defenders of the realm would not be out in force today, as she had seen at least two of them at the concert. If Adolf Hitler planned to invade, this would be the time to do it, with the diversion of a school choir leaving the coast abandoned.

Judy's giggle froze at the sight of the mutilated beach below her. The barbed wire defences completely covered the shore now, and a fence had been erected to prevent people like her from wandering down the little rocky paths that led down to the sand. A sign accosted her: DANGER! MINES. Beneath the words was a crudely drawn skull and crossbones to ram the point home.

It was as though the wire had a life of its own and were creeping its way over the sand, up across the rocky paths, and would eventually engulf the entire school grounds. Part of her already felt like a prisoner. The girls were the distracted guests on the *Titanic*, singing their little ditties for the grown-ups, making their beds with the counterpane folded carefully back, digging for victory, preparing for mathematics examinations the teacher would not even discuss . . . and all the while, the Germans were closing in.

The war was being lost; she could not be sure of it, but her father's letters grew ever more guarded. She knew he accepted that there would be an invasion; it was impossible even for him to dismiss it any longer, and he was afraid. That was why he always sounded so impatient with her in his letters. He was afraid, and his fear was making him honest with her for the first time she could remember. His last letter to her would have been positively thrilling if it had not also been so macabre, the ghastly details of an invasion plan interlaced with indignation at her latest acts of disobedience.

> Since you refuse to desist, I should perhaps put your mind at rest that I have laid in place plans for your welfare in the event of an invasion. I truly hope you did not imagine I would neglect such a task. Should such a dark day occur for our country, I have gained the assurance of one of your teachers that he will take care of you, as I will almost certainly be unable to discharge my duty to you at such a time.
>
> However, I must impress upon you yet again that whether the Germans choose to invade is Mr Churchill's problem, not yours. I should rather you concentrated your tiny mind on the small matter of your education and the

improvement of your reprehensible behaviour. I received yet another letter from your headmistress last week, in which she informed me that she had seen fit to reprimand you for breaking the uniform rules and that you had had the cheek to engage her in an argument. At your age, you really ought to be ashamed to have earned a punishment for any reason at all, but mindless insolence is unacceptable under any circumstances. I sincerely hope that trinket of yours was not the cause of the offence.

Judy fingered the trinket in question, which had indeed been the cause of the altercation and subsequent explosion of violence from Miss Miller, but her father's habitual use of the word "trinket" cut her to the core. It was the sign that she was a marked girl—no, a marked woman—and her father knew it, or he would not have put plans in place for her care. Plans he would not share with her. Judy kicked the soft, moist earth in indignation. He had not even considered telling her to whom she had been entrusted, though it was obviously Mr Peterson, since he had been a de facto guardian to her for so long. Why could he not have told her that?

There was another escapee in the vicinity; Judy could hear the rustle of twigs underfoot in the nearby undergrowth and knew without a doubt that she was hearing the sound of guilty feet. And it was not just because whoever it was must have known he was out-of-bounds; Judy's fellow miscreant was also bunking off the school concert, and she felt an overpowering urge to seek him out, if nothing else because there had to be a certain safety in numbers.

Perhaps I will end up living like this, thought Judy as she ducked to avoid the low-hanging branch of a horse chestnut tree. *When the Germans come I shall hide away among the trees, and Father's chosen patron will bring me food parcels under cover of darkness*. But Judy had little time to extrapolate further. The miscreant was farther ahead of her than she had realised. As she emerged into open space again, the beach a little closer now, Judy saw the figure in question and flinched with shock. The woman had slipped under the fence and lowered herself gingerly onto a narrow rocky shelf that almost completely sheltered her from view. This was too dangerous even for Judy, and she opened her mouth to call out to the trespasser and warn her to come back, only to close it again and step back into the protective cover of the undergrowth.

The figure—too far away to identify—was carrying a knapsack of some kind slung over one shoulder and obviously knew exactly what she was doing. Judy held her breath, straining for any sound that might give away what the woman was playing at, since she did not dare poke her head out to look. There were low sounds of fumbling and rustling and the clicking and unclicking of metal clasps, after which Judy heard the unmistakable sounds of a camera at work, the repeated clicks and creaking noises of shutters opening and closing.

Judy was too frightened to feel any excitement. She had just about enough common sense to know she had not been meant to witness this and would be in serious trouble if the woman turned around and realised she was being watched. But it was no easy business to escape with twigs all over the ground that might crackle and draw the woman's attention to the unwelcome presence of a spy. *Keep your head*, Judy told herself, inching her way with painful slowness back in the direction of the school. She bit her lip as the thin branches of the low-hanging trees scratched her bare arms with her every backward step, willing herself not to make a sound. It was bad enough that the tiny, unavoidable debris of the trees crackled underfoot however carefully she stepped. *Keep calm; she did not hear you or see you coming. She won't see you leave.*

Only when Judy was certain she was out of sight did she turn and run hell-for-leather back onto the school grounds. She was forming a plan in her mind to make her way to the Petersons' cottage. She could hide out there until the Petersons came home and then tell them everything, certain that they would know what to do. Judy knew she would be missed as soon as the concert finished; she might already have been, but there was nothing any teacher could do about it until after the concert, which would be prolonged by applause and an encore and further applause and endless chatter in the hall afterwards as refreshments were served.

As she bolted to the cottage gate, Judy was startled by the sight of another figure walking towards her from the direction of the school building. She knew from the way the tall, lean figure bobbed slightly at every step that it was Mr Forbes on some errand or other and felt an immediate sense of relief. If she could explain the situation quickly enough, they might be able to catch Miss Miller in the act of photographing the coastal defences, and she would not have to find a way to prove her mad theory after all.

Mr Forbes, however, was not looking desperately cooperative. His normally mild expression darkened at the sight of Judy bouncing towards him, but she was too caught up in the case at hand to notice. "Mr Forbes, come quickly!" she called, breathlessly, hurrying to his side. "Please, there's something you must see!"

Mr Forbes pressed a finger to his lips, hissing at her to be quiet. "What do you think you're doing out of the concert? You should be on that stage halfway through *The Ash Grove* by now!"

"Miss Miller's taking pictures!" Judy put in, as there was clearly no time to introduce the subject gently. "She's gone under the wire with a camera."

"Oh, don't be ridiculous!" he snapped, chivvying her in the direction of the school building. "I have just seen Miss Miller walk back into the hall. You've had plenty of time to think up a story. Is that really the best you could do?"

"Please, she really is!" Judy protested, wriggling to free herself, but Mr Forbes' fingers tightened around her arm, making escape or further conversation impossible. She gasped with pain. "I . . . I really did see her. I'm sure it was her!"

"Now you listen to me!" he barked, in a tone she was not used to hearing from him. "I think this little fantasy of yours has gone on quite long enough. I dare say you've been reading any manner of stories about Jerry spies hiding under the bed and disguising themselves as nuns and nurses and the like, but this has now gone too far."

"You're hurting me!" she whimpered, placing her free hand over his. "Please let go!"

He immediately let go of her, making some distance between them. "Sorry," he said numbly, "but I do wish you'd stop this nonsense. Miss Miller is safely seated in the hall by now; I saw her walk that way myself. You had no business slipping out of the concert. You've got yourself into very hot water."

Judy scurried after him in alarm. She could not help noticing how quickly he was moving in the direction of the school; he really could not get her through the door quickly enough. "Oh, please don't tell on me. That really would be beastly of you!"

Another mistake. Forbes' face was stormy again, but Judy was too naive to realise the nerve she had just hit with him. "I do not *tell* on you, and I hardly care how beastly you think me for doing my job!" he snapped, with uncharacteristic ill temper. "I am the teacher; you are the pupil. Be so kind as to remember your—to remember that."

He had been about to say "your place", and Judy knew it. She blushed with shame. "I'm sorry," she said quietly, avoiding looking at him. She almost choked on the word. "Sir."

"As it happens, I have no intention of referring you to anyone. I have put a great deal of time and effort into your education, and I will not allow you to throw away a chance by getting yourself expelled. Just do yourself a favour and keep your childish little stories to yourself."

"Sir, *please*!" she pleaded. A valuable moment had been lost; Miss Miller would certainly have finished her work by now and might even be on her way back to the concert hall so that no one would know what she had been up to. If Judy could only make him listen . . . "It's not a story, sir; you know it's not! I saw her!"

"Judy," he said severely, "one more word out of you, and I will hand you over to Miss Miller myself. I have no idea what you're talking about, but Miss Miller has not left the building. Whomever you imagine you saw, it was not her. Do you understand?"

Judy nodded wretchedly, her eyes misting over, but she would never give in to tears in front of him. She shook her head violently and plucked up the courage to look at Forbes, but she was unsettled to see that he looked anxious rather than angry. "What is it?" she asked quietly. "Why are you looking at me like that?"

Forbes coloured. "It's nothing. I have just noticed something, that's all. It's not important."

It was fortunate that she was too preoccupied to press him further; it would have been too complicated for him to explain precisely what he had noticed: when her face was flushed like that from running, it accentuated her colouring in a way he would not normally have acknowledged, and there was no pretending otherwise. Even without that little gold star around her neck, Judy looked unmistakably foreign, and nothing on earth would conceal it if danger came. Every tiny detail of her face that ought to have marked her out as a beauty would count against her, from the glossy black curls to the vast brown eyes, those tiny markers that spoke of an ancient people scattered to the four corners of the earth.

"It's all right, Judy; I don't want her to have to know," he said, recovering himself. "Here's what you are going to do. You are going to slip back to the changing rooms and get back into your uniform." He took the pencil and small leather-bound notebook he kept in his inner jacket pocket and began scrawling a complex equation. "Then, I want you to solve this for me," he said as he wrote. "It should keep you out of mischief for a little while."

Judy took the paper from him and grimaced. "This will take me hours," she said blankly. "When do you want it?"

"Slip it under the staff room door before you retire tonight," he said. "I will look at it in the morning."

"But I'll miss supper," she said plaintively, "or I shall never finish it before evening roll call!"

Forbes shrugged his shoulders. "I daresay it won't be the first time. Think of the alternative." With that, he limped away, leaving Judy to creep back into the school building yet again and get herself changed, hopefully without anyone noticing. Then it was back up the stairs and along the echoing corridor to the cold, dark, empty library she was coming to associate with being perpetually in disgrace.

10

The library was the perfect location for a little self-pity. There was something about the sombre atmosphere that reflected Judy's own sense of gloom: the rows and rows of leather-bound books all around her bore witness to the passing of time and the many generations who had written and studied and slipped into history, leaving behind so little of their thoughts and discoveries. It may have been merely that children do not play and lark around in a library, but it felt adult to Judy, full of possible journeys into the past, as close as possible to a place where the great minds of human civilisation meet together as equals.

Not that any of it could matter now, in the middle of a war about to be lost. Judy stared down at the white page, on which she had drawn a row of swirly snails, a row of six-pointed stars and an intricate sprawl of cobwebs . . . but not a single digit had found its way there. She could not bring herself to look out the window, knowing that the girls would be out enjoying the recreation hour before supper by now. She could hear the murmur of skipping feet and chatter and felt a familiar surge of resentment—that Mr Forbes, of all people, should have refused to listen to her! He was supposed to be on *her* side! Pulling rank like that—it was so silly. He was not like the other teachers anyhow. It was like a young man growing a beard to try to prove how grown-up he was and merely looking like the infant son of a garden gnome.

The door opened with an irritating whine, and Ursula Hamilton trotted in, cradling three large volumes in her plump arms. Judy was a past master at making enemies, and Ursula had had a tendency to wind her up since they had found themselves with adjoining beds on their very first night at the school. Ursula had dropped Judy in it over a jar of contraband mint humbugs, and Judy had retaliated by emptying out the tin of biscuits Ursula had hidden under her bed and replacing them with a large spider. The arachnid had been sporting enough to crawl up Ursula's sleeve after lights-out, when she had opened the tin in search of an illicit snack. Never had the dorm echoed with such bloodcurdling screams of panic.

A lot of water had gone under the bridge since those cantankerous days, but the two girls still glared at one another with undisguised suspicion across the library. "Got yourself into trouble again?" enquired Ursula, dropping the books onto the nearest table with a maddening crash. "Now *there's* a surprise."

"Mind your own business," Judy retorted. It was a lame response. She should have thought up some devastating reply that would have taken Ursy down a peg or two, but her heart was not in it this afternoon. "I've some maths to finish, if you must know."

Ursula snorted like a small constipated piglet. "He fancies you, you know. Everyone says so."

Judy felt herself reddening for the second time that day. "Don't be ridiculous! He's always cross with me these days. Everyone is." Judy always found it so difficult to hide her emotions, and the other girl knew it; she could sense Ursula enjoying her awkwardness and knew she would see it as proof that her theory was correct. "He's a teacher. It wouldn't be allowed."

Ursula's watery grey eyes rolled with the effort of sustaining a conversation with one of her inferiors. "Oh, come on, Jude, that's obviously not true. You're sixteen. You know you're allowed to get married."

Judy swallowed hard. She knew Ursula was after a reaction, preferably a reaction strong enough to warrant the intervention of a teacher and Judy's public humiliation, but for once Judy was determined to resist. "I have to finish my pun—my prep."

Ursula threw back her head, squealing with triumphant laughter. "I knew it! I knew you were in trouble! What daft antics have you been up to this time?"

Red mist swirled before Judy's eyes. "Why don't you just buzz off?" There, that had sounded quite calm, she told herself. Judy picked up her pencil and drew a few skulls and crossbones beneath her other doodles. She was going to keep her cool if it killed her.

"Oooooh!" Ursula exclaimed, with mock surprise. "Somebody's getting angry, somebody's getting angry . . ."

Red mist turned blue. A deep, dark, swirling, sticky, staining blue. The inkwell, full almost to the brim with ink, happened to be the nearest object to Judy's shaking fingers. In one deft movement, she pulled it out of the desk and hurled it in Ursula's direction, striking her squarely in the chest. The girl stood in stunned silence, blue ink splashed all over her crisp, starched blouse, a small cluster of blue freckles gathering on her nose and cheek. If the ink had been red,

Ursula would have looked as though she had been shot at close range by an expert marksman and was seconds from expiring.

The rush of exhilaration immediately gave way to panic in Judy as Ursula screamed loud enough to bring the entire nation to her defence. It was spider time all over again. "You've got a screw loose!" she shouted. "You have; everyone says so! They ought to lock you up!"

Judy was half-tempted to give up and make a run for it. If she bolted out the door immediately, she would be well out of the way of the school building within minutes, but she knew there was nowhere left for her to hide now. She could not possibly run for help to a friendly teacher with Ursula covered in indelible ink; it would have been regarded as an unspeakable thing to do if she had been ten, let alone sixteen. "Stop it!" Judy almost pleaded. "It's not that bad. Stop screaming!"

But Ursula was still screaming at the top of her voice when Matron stepped through the door to enquire as to the source of the commotion. "Oh, do pull yourself together, girl!" barked Matron, silencing Ursula immediately. She looked the girl up and down, noting the large blots of ink all over her clothes, before turning to face the culprit. To Judy's horror, Matron did not look the least bit enraged with her. If anything, she was looking at her a little too much like Mr Forbes had done.

"What's the meaning of this, Judith?" she asked quietly, looking down at her as though desperate for there to be an innocent explanation. "What do you think you're doing?"

"She was teasing me, Matron," answered Judy unsteadily, but it sounded pathetically childish. "I lost my temper and threw my inkwell at her."

Faced with anyone else, Judy might have braced herself, but she knew Matron was incapable of so much as raising her voice. Judy felt her eyes growing hot; Ursula seemed to have sensed that the situation was a great deal worse than she had anticipated, and she shuffled quietly away. Matron did not turn to look at her as she said, "Ursula, my dear, I think you had better return to your dormitory for a change of clothes. We'll see what is to be done about your uniform. Run along now."

When Ursula had slipped out of the library, Judy found her voice. "I'm sorry, Matron. I'm sorry. I never mean to make such a mess of everything."

Matron touched the girl's shoulder. "If this were a first offence, it would be a different matter, but you know nobody can help you this time."

"I'm going to be expelled, aren't I?"

"I'm not sure Miss Miller has much choice, Judy. You have had so many warnings. Come on now, stand up straight and take it like a big girl. You'd better come with me."

It was a long walk from the library to Miss Miller's study, along a narrow corridor lined with photographs of school groups past, down a flight of stairs, along yet another corridor, past the chapel, past the staff room and the men's staff room, past the parlour and up the infinitely long, grandiose central staircase, at the top of which lay Miss Miller's study and the scene of Judy's worst childhood memories. Judy and Matron walked in complete silence; it must have been time to retire to the dormitories because there were mercifully few people for them to pass, and Judy was aware only of the tapping of two pairs of shoes touching the wooden floorboards and the swish of Matron's many petticoats with every step. The strange thing was, it was not Miss Miller's anger she was afraid of facing, or even her father's when it came to it—though she did not fancy the welcome she would get when she arrived home with her school trunk and yet another letter from her headmistress. It was the thought of all the people who had tried so hard to keep her on the straight and narrow—Matron and Mr Forbes and the Petersons. The Petersons more than anyone. She wondered whether she would be allowed to say good-bye to Annie before she left, but she was not sure she would be able to face any of them now. She would do the cowardly thing and slip away if she could, back to the anonymity of London. Anything she could bring herself to say would have to be written in a long letter she might never even pluck up the courage to post.

"Perhaps you had better let me do the talking," Matron suggested gently as she knocked on the door. "You needn't say anything unless she asks you a question."

"It's better," murmured Judy, hanging back in spite of herself as the door opened. "Though short of killing me, there's not much worse she can do." Judy swallowed a wave of queasiness, as she had done many times over the years in that place, and followed Matron into the room.

Another fragment of memory, a moment frozen in time when it was almost too late but perhaps not quite. There would still have been the remotest of chances that things might have ended differently. She could have found some way to tell Mr Peterson or Mr Forbes what she pieced together in that room whilst Miss Miller was passing sentence against her. She could have saddled someone else with the responsibility for what happened next.

"So here we are at last, Miss Randall," said Miss Miller

from behind her desk. "I think we both knew it would come to this sooner or later. In spite of the best efforts of your teachers and the numerous chances you have been given, you have shown yourself to be wholly unworthy of your place at this school."

The only puzzling detail about the safe behind Miss Miller's desk was that it was there at all. Everyone had secrets, and headmistresses must have many, she thought, papers and perhaps money that needed to be kept locked away. It was just that the safe had not been there before Christmas. Few girls ever darkened the doors of Miss Miller's study more than a couple of times during their school days. Once was usually enough to put the fear of God in anyone, and teachers who came and went did not count. Adults never noticed anything, particularly these days, when they were always whispering in corners, worrying about everything. Judy had been in this room, forced to stand in this very position hundreds of times over the years, and she knew the room's every detail.

". . . a despicable contempt for all authority, an unwillingness to obey the rules. Every attempt to discipline you and bring you into line has failed."

Judy had seen Miss Miller open the safe on one previous occasion, when she had assumed that Judy was too busy hugging her mangled hands to take any notice; but pain and anxiety had the effect of sharpening Judy's powers of observation, not diminishing them. The only trouble was that she had seen nothing in her brief glimpse into the safe that could possibly be of interest. Papers. Just papers. Bills perhaps or her diary, items that were personal but unimportant.

"It is not without some regret that I must ask you to leave

this school. On the rare occasions on which I am forced to expel a pupil, I would normally summon the staff, but in this situation, I think it would be better if you left as discreetly as possible."

The camera film must be in there, thought Judy. *The film . . .* But even Judy's obsessive mind began to blur at the unavoidable reality of what she was hearing. Her school life was over. She had been expelled. There could be no more education, no Oxford and quite possibly no home to go back to. She did not know what her father would do when he received the news: she could not imagine him kicking her out of the house, but nor could she imagine him allowing her to live with him in London. She had wanted more than anything to leave her school days behind but on her terms or at least on good terms.

"Do you have anything to say?"

Judy was aware that there had been a lengthy silence she had failed to notice, and Miss Miller expected some sort of response from her. "I understand, madam."

Miss Miller's eyes narrowed. "I think an apology might be in order, don't you?"

Judy drew in a short, sharp breath that caused her eyes to well up. "I'm sorry about the ink. I'm sorry I lost my temper."

The halfhearted apology for what had been one of the least of Judy's transgressions was more than compensated for by the tears that began to course down the girl's face. She bowed her head so that her hair concealed her face as much as possible, but her shoulders heaved with the effort to control herself. "You will go directly to your dormitory. You will not converse with anyone on the way, and you will remain there. Tomorrow morning, I will send a telegram to your father, advising him of the unfortunate situation, and arrangements will be made to convey you to the railway station."

Judy nodded but could not raise her head. "I shall go and pack."

"Matron, I trust that you will escort Judith to her dormitory when she has had a moment to compose herself."

"Of course, Miss Miller. I shall take her there myself."

Matron put her arm around Judy's shoulders and led her carefully out into the corridor, closely followed by Miss Miller, who brushed past them with an air of triumph. Judy turned and pressed her forehead against the wall. "Might I have a moment alone?" she asked plaintively. "I can find my own way to the dormitory; I know my way round the school."

"Of course; take your time." Matron took several steps away, then turned back anxiously. "You aren't going to do anything silly, are you?" she asked awkwardly. "It's not the end of the world, though it probably feels that way at the moment."

"I know. I'll be all right."

Judy listened carefully for the sound of Matron's retreating footsteps down the stairs. When the corridor was in complete silence, she counted to five before wiping the tears from her face, glancing around to ensure that she was truly alone and slipping back into Miss Miller's study.

The shock of being expelled worked in her favour—she *had* to prove her crazy theory before the night was out, and since she had just been handed the ultimate sanction, she no longer felt afraid. If Miss Miller caught her in her study, there was little more she could do to Judy short of calling the police, and Judy doubted that Miss Miller would want the scandal of a pupil being arrested on the premises.

It was always useful to have a way with numbers. She may have seen the safe opened only once, but one glance had been enough time for her to memorise the number: 1-8-9-8. It was obviously some date or other, but Judy had other thoughts swirling around her head as she turned the dial of the safe four times, stifling a squeak of excitement when the door obediently opened.

~

Peterson and Forbes had been sitting in their staffroom for half an hour when Matron put her head around the door and told them about Judy's expulsion. Judy had been a distracting enough topic of conversation before Matron had broken the news; after she left, they both abandoned their marking and could talk of nothing else. Forbes had just lit a cigarette when the condemned female herself tumbled through the door like a thing possessed.

"Good evening, Judy," said Peterson gravely. "I am very sorry to hear the news."

"Oh, never mind about that!" gasped Judy, rushing up to his desk. "I must show you something. I found it—"

"Never mind?" thundered Peterson, snatching the reading glasses off his face like a street fighter removing his gloves. "Have you taken leave of your senses?"

It was a pointless question to ask someone like Judy, Peterson mused, glancing at the absurd sight of a young woman who still had ink all over her fingers, shoelaces trailing the floor and a mop of hair that had not seen a comb or a hairpin in days. She had never had any sense from which to part company. He noticed the folded letter she was clutching in one hand. "Judy, what's that?"

"I can't read it; it's in German," she said breathlessly. "But I know it's important. I thought perhaps you could translate it for me."

Peterson took the letter from her and began to read it. He knew Judy would be scrutinising his face for any reaction and endeavoured to remain calm. "Where did you get this?" It was no good; the hostile tone put Judy on her guard immediately, and she put her head down. "Answer me, girl! Where did you get this?"

"Miss Miller's safe. I never thought of it because it seemed such an obvious place to hide a secret, but then I thought—"

"You broke into Miss Miller's safe?"

"Oh no, nothing like that. I noted the number and opened it. I'm good with numbers."

"Don't split hairs. You took this from her safe?"

"Yes."

Judy felt the pressure of an invisible hand tightening around her throat, squeezing the breath out of her body. Peterson was staring fixedly at her, the letter trembling very slightly in his hands; if she had not known better, she would have said he was frightened. "Do you understand how serious this is? Do you even truly understand what it is?"

"I thought it was proof," said Judy softly, but she was unsettled by the sense that she was out of her depth. There was something about the way he was looking at her, the sudden tone of urgency that made her want desperately for him to roll his eyes and tell her she was being silly as usual.

133

"That is exactly what it is," he retorted. "It's exactly what you wanted. The proof that Miss Miller is indeed working for the Germans. Do you not understand how serious this is?"

Judy looked to Mr Forbes for reassurance, but his face was ashen. "Oughtn't we to call the police?"

"This is an isolated school, Judy," said Peterson. "A police car would take at least twenty minutes driving down those narrow roads without lights. Even if I can reach a telephone without being overheard, it may be too late by the time they arrive."

"Might she escape?" asked Judy. "Couldn't we . . . I don't know, detain her in some way?"

Peterson rose to his feet, holding the letter up as though exhibiting the first piece of evidence at a murder trial. "What do you suppose the first thing is that a spy does when she is discovered?" He waited only a second for a response. "She removes all evidence of her activities. Even if that means eliminating the witness."

Forbes was at Judy's side in an instant. "Look here, this is all getting very melodramatic. Is there no way we could replace the letter in the safe before Miss Miller checks it? If the letter is in its proper place, she may not know Judy has found her out."

"First of all, it is too risky. There is every chance we would be seen entering or leaving the study. And it is too late. Look at your hands, Judy."

Judy looked at her fingers, which were still stained heavily with the ink she had thrown at Ursula Hamilton. She could see the inky fingerprints she had made on the back of the letter without noticing. "I'm not cut out for this, am I?"

she whimpered. "And she'll know it's me anyway, because I was the last one in her room. I never thought further than opening that safe."

"Is there any way we could hide her in your cottage?" asked Forbes. "Just until we are able to summon the police?"

Peterson shook his head impatiently. "The path to the cottage is in full view of every window this side of the school, including the headmistress' study. In any case, it would be the first place she'd look."

"I'll make a run for it," said Judy firmly. "You know I can run. If I can get as far as the constabulary—"

"Forget it, Judy. It's far too dangerous, running through the undergrowth after dusk and so close to the coast. You'd be lucky if some idiot didn't start taking pot shots at you." Peterson made a sudden stride towards her, causing her to shrink back involuntarily. "I'm sorry, Judy, but there's no time for all this talk. You have to be safely out of sight. I have no idea where Miss Miller is now, and she cannot get anywhere near you."

He pushed her backwards in the direction of the storage cupboard he had not found much use for until that moment and turned the key that rested in the lock. "Please!" she hissed, too startled to scream. "I'm awfully claustrophobic. Please don't!"

"I'm sorry; I'm afraid you're going to have to pull yourself together about that," answered Peterson, assisting her into the large empty confines of the cupboard. It was not nearly large enough in Judy's opinion, and she found herself struggling to avoid it. "Don't," he said quietly. "I'm sorry this is a little drastic, but I cannot risk removing you from this room in case you are seen, and this is the safest place I can think of." He felt her shaking against his arm and knelt down next to her. "Take deep breaths. You're perfectly safe. There is plenty of ventilation at the top; you won't suffocate. But you must keep calm. I'll get you out as soon as I can summon help."

"I wish you could lock her up," said Judy miserably as he carefully closed the door and locked it, placing the key in his breast pocket.

"So do I," answered Peterson out loud. He went back to his desk, opened a drawer and retrieved another key, which he handed to Forbes. "That's the other copy of the key in case you need to get her out."

Forbes put the key away. "What the hell do we do now?"

"We keep calm," answered Peterson tonelessly. "I am going to the cottage to use the telephone. It will take me about ten minutes to get there, as I can't risk rushing, which means we have half an hour at least before the police arrive. If Elsa doesn't notice the safe has been opened, we have nothing to fear."

"And if she does?"

"Focus your mind on the here and now, old man. Under no circumstances leave this room. I will return as soon as I have put a call through to the police. Check Judy after ten minutes but do not let her out, however much she protests. I'm not sure she appreciates the danger she's in."

"The letter?"

"I have it."

A familiar rhythm of impatient footsteps approached them, quickly followed by a hammering on the door. Peterson gestured to Forbes to sit at his desk and walked over to let

Miss Miller in. She walked directly past Peterson into the centre of the room. "I trust you have heard the news?" she demanded, glancing in Forbes' direction as he rose to his feet. "Please don't trouble yourself to get up, Mr Forbes," she added with a smirk. "It must be irksome for a man such as you."

Forbes sat down heavily, forcing himself not to look in the direction of the cupboard. "We have heard that Judith has been expelled, yes."

"She has run away," said Miss Miller. "I left her with Matron outside my study. When I returned ten minutes later, they had gone, and I assumed Matron had taken her to her dormitory as I instructed. I have just visited the dormitory, only to discover Matron in a state because the little beast has run off."

"Why ever would she do that if she knows she will be leaving anyway?" enquired Forbes. "It seems a little irrational."

"This is Judith Randall we're talking about, my good man; of course it's irrational," Miss Miller put in. "According to Matron, she left without packing a thing. Just bolted."

"Well, in that case she won't have gone far," said Peterson calmly. "She'll have run off into the night in a fit of pique. I'll walk over to the cottage now and see if she has gone there. If Mary hasn't seen her, I'll call the police."

"I doubt they'll be much interested in a runaway schoolgirl," said Miss Miller quickly. "She's sixteen, not six."

"Yes," said Peterson, shepherding her out of the room, "but it's late, and a young girl should not be out alone like that."

"The little minx will come back as soon as she gets tired

and hungry," Miss Miller assured him. "She's not had supper. She was being punished for some other transgression when she attacked Ursula."

"Well, I shan't call the police if you think I'm overreacting," said Peterson. "But I will look and see if she has skulked off to the cottage. She may just have wanted to tell Annie everything. Why don't you stroll over with me?"

The idea was forming in Peterson's mind that if he could lure Elsa away from the main building to the more relaxed environment of his home, he might be able to keep her distracted for so long that, after a long, relaxing conversation, she might not feel like returning to her study again that evening. It was a risky strategy, as he knew she had everything to lose by confessing, even to him, and he had no way of knowing how she would respond. "It's getting very late," he added. "Why don't you come over to the house? If Judy's not there, Annie may have seen her—"

"Thank you, no," answered Miss Miller curtly. "I would not dream of imposing on Mrs Peterson at this late hour. If you find Judy, I trust that you will send her directly to me. There are one or two little details I need to tidy up with her before she goes."

"Of course," promised Peterson. He watched as Miss Miller turned on her heel and walked away in the direction of her study. There was a dogmatic tone even to her footsteps, he thought, before hurrying as quickly as he dared in the direction of home.

He had given away too much, he realised, just in that one friendly invitation to come to the cottage. However much he had attempted to dress it up as a practical solution to a problem, she had known instinctively that he was up to something. It was an awkward fact that in the long years the Petersons had taught at the school, they had never once invited Elsa into their home, and the sudden suggestion that she should enter their hallowed domain had put her on her guard. But then, her determination to keep the police off the premises had spoken for itself as well.

The police would come, Peterson reassured himself. Even outside, he dared not pick up his pace too much in case he was being observed, and there was a piece of information he had refrained from sharing with either Forbes or Judy: Elsa was not acting alone. The letter had referred to another source, about whom all he knew was that she was female, and an unknown enemy was more terrifying than even Elsa Miller on a mission. At least he knew Elsa; he had some sense —perhaps more than anyone else—of why she was doing this. But an invisible enemy hardly bore thinking about. He did not have long to keep Judy safe, he told himself. Half an hour and no longer.

⁓

Judy sat in the darkness with her eyes shut tight and tried every trick she knew to keep herself calm. When she was little, her nanny had told her nursery rhymes to distract her when she had woken up screaming in the middle of the night. It had been dark then too, almost as dark as in this cupboard.

The owl and the pussycat went to sea in a beautiful pea-green boat . . .

She wriggled slightly to get herself into a more comfort-able position, and her foot touched the corner of the cupboard, warning her of just how narrow the space was. Judy felt her body shaking, and no silly little words from child-hood were ever going to distract her from where she was and what she had done. She was locked in a tiny space, held into place by thick, impenetrable walls of wood. They had locked her up, and she did not entirely understand why.

This was her nightmare of what the future held, coming back to haunt her again. The future, just weeks or even just days away, when the Germans would come, when the Nazis would come crawling all over the country and there would be nowhere left to run. She would have to become invisible like this, concealed in some dark underworld of backrooms and cellars and abandoned buildings where fugitives hide away, ever in fear of discovery.

Fear. It was only in the stifling darkness that it occurred to her how little she had ever truly been afraid before now. Anxious, certainly, many times: when she had been late, when she had been forgetful or untidy or insolent, when her father had raised his voice to her or when she had stood outside Miss Miller's study awaiting retribution. But those were mere schoolgirl jitters. Even when her mother's health had gone into rapid decline and Judy had been warned to expect the worst, she had been too young to take it all in and never felt the fear of losing the person who constituted her entire world. There had been no fear afterwards, just a numb sense of rage that her mother was gone.

But this was real, adult fear, tearing at her from the inside out like a ravenous animal. She had done something terri-ble. She could not fully comprehend it; Judy knew only that she had blundered in such a disastrous fashion this time that someone might actually get hurt. She imagined doing things differently. All the moments of the term when she had been commanded to cease and desist stretched out before her like a series of reprieves she had refused to accept.

Judy could hear movement on the other side of the door and had no way of knowing who had entered the room. She forced her head between her knees to stifle any sound that might come out of her mouth, willing the tide of panic not to rise again. There were voices talking, but the heavy wooden cupboard was virtually soundproof, and she could not make out a word of what was being said or even who was talking. The indistinct murmur continued for several minutes like a maddening buzz of insects on the other side of a windowpane; then she heard footsteps approaching. One, two, three . . . the door opened quietly, but Judy felt a cry escaping her throat.

The intruder must have expected such a response and threw himself down, slapping a hand over her mouth. It was Mr Forbes. "Shh!" he instructed, kneeling by her side. "It's nothing to worry about. Mr Peterson is back from his house."

"Are the police coming?" she whispered. She attempted to crawl out, but Mr Forbes put a hand on her shoulder to stop her. "Oh, please let me out! I'd sooner try my luck running for it than sitting cooped up in here!"

"I'm sure you would, Judy," said Mr Peterson, appearing behind Mr Forbes, "but you must sit tight a little longer. The police won't come until morning."

"This is madness," said Mr Forbes, looking back at his friend. "Morning will be too late."

"They're hopelessly short of constables with so many men being called up," Peterson tried to explain, "and I'm afraid

I may not have put the case very well. It all sounds so improbably mad when one tries to explain the situation. A respectable headmistress is passing information to Jerry and may well be a danger to the public now that she's been exposed. If the story were published in *Boy's Own*, I'd think it far-fetched."

"I have to stay in here all night?" squeaked Judy. She made another attempt at escape, but Mr Forbes proved to be a very resistant wall between her and the outside world.

"No you don't. I'll think of something," promised Peterson, crouching down to her level. "But you must stay put for the moment, and please, please don't make a sound." He reached into his pocket and pulled out a set of rosary beads. "Here, say a decade or two," he suggested, handing it to her. "It'll take your mind off things. Now I'm going to have to lock you in again, I'm afraid. Deep breaths."

With that, he pushed the door shut as cautiously as possible, turning the key in the lock. He looked back and saw Forbes placing an unlit cigarette in his mouth. "Sorry, old chap," said Forbes, removing it to speak. "Just trying to relax."

"Don't," said Peterson. "The smoke might make Judy cough in there. If I can't get the police to come out, I shall have to find some way to spirit her away to the cottage. I just can't think of a way to remove her without the risk of her being seen, but she can't sit in that cupboard all night, and it feels peculiar keeping her locked in there anyway."

"What do you want to do?" asked Forbes, fingering the cigarette nervously. "I only wish one of us had a car."

"I'm going to go over to the north wing and use the telephone there. It will take me a little longer walking through those corridors in the dark, but I can't keep going back and forth to and from the cottage. It looks too suspicious."

"Peterson, it looks suspicious enough already," Forbes put in, unhelpfully. "We're never normally here this late, even when we're very busy."

"All right. Stay where you are. If I cannot get the police to come out, we will have to proceed to the cottage together with Judy and hope for the best. Don't move from here until I return."

Forbes sat back down at his desk, which was beginning to feel more and more like a sentry post. "No disrespect, Peterson—you're a good man—but do you really believe Judy is in any danger? She's only a girl. Even if Miss Miller is working for the Germans, surely the most she'll do if she knows the game's up is to run away. She could go into hiding."

"Harry, don't be so naive," answered Peterson tersely. "The woman is a Nazi. She may already know that Judy is in possession of the one piece of evidence that she is a traitor. If she doesn't, it's only a matter of time before she checks, and I know her well enough to understand what that means. Elsa will have been instructed to kill anyone who threatens to expose her."

"But does she really have it in her? I just can't imagine her actually doing it. Pulling the trigger, I mean."

Peterson moved closer to the door, partly to listen in case anyone approached the room from the corridor and partly to stay away from the cupboard. He could not be sure how much Judy could hear. "Oh, I can, I'm afraid," he said. "As far as Elsa and her friends in Germany are concerned, Judy is a Jewess. Her life is worthless, and despatching her from the world is no more wicked than shooting a dog. And Elsa grew up surrounded by death. She's seen it many times before. She may well have already killed."

～

Peterson was not a man who could be termed fanciful or excitable by nature, but the dimly lit corridors and stairwells chilled him to the bone as he crept along, treading as lightly as possible. It was hard to imagine a more sinister place than a quiet, empty building that by day was teeming with life. He did not need to feel his way in the dark, as he knew every crevice of the school and anticipated each step, every loose board as he walked along, pausing from time to time to ensure that he was not being followed.

The narrow, winding stone staircase at the entrance to the north wing filled him with particular misgivings, as it was impossible to see if anyone was coming up the other way until it was too late, and the stone steps magnified his every footfall. As he descended into the claustrophobic darkness of the stairwell, Peterson found himself surrounded by faces, almost as though they had been summoned by a wordless command. It was the stress of holding a life in his hands again, the sense of being caught up in a chain of events over which he had no control. He only ever found himself back in that place when he was frightened or unsettled, but he could not give in to it now. He felt the sharp metal teeth of a barbed wire fence tearing at his flesh as he threw himself against it, saw those faces staring at him through the long dark corridors of memory, accusing, lamenting . . . He paused at the foot of the stairs, allowing himself the brief luxury of closing his eyes.

Please go, he willed them, *please go*, but when he opened his eyes, he was surrounded by the shadows of women and children he remembered; those sad, thin, desperate faces, gazing at him as though he knew the way out of the labyrinth into which they had been lured. He clenched his fists until his arms shook with the effort; he felt the sudden pain of a metal-tipped boot slamming into his shin and held his breath to prevent himself from crying out.

Peterson was alone again in an empty passageway, near a nook in which a telephone was nestled, awaiting the sound of his voice. He marched the final four steps to the telephone, gave a last glance about him and lifted the receiver.

~

Forbes glanced at the old carriage clock over the fireplace, calculating the minutes Peterson had been away. No more than ten minutes, but he felt the burden of being alone. It was about time he checked on Judy anyway; the brief contact with her would distract him from the thought that there was a devotee of Adolf Hitler on the premises. He ought really to wait until Peterson's return, but there was no sound at all from the corridor, and there was no way of knowing if Miss Miller was still at the school. For all they knew, she might have cut and run, given up on retrieving the letter and found her way to some place of safety, though he could not imagine where she would find shelter in these parts.

Forbes moved towards the cupboard, glancing constantly at the door that led out to the corridor. If he opened the left-hand door of the cupboard, it would be impossible to see inside from the other end of the room if someone did walk in, and he could quite easily close and lock the door, claiming that he had been searching for something. He made one final pause and opened the cupboard.

Judy was curled up with her back leaning against the side panel, her arms clasped together holding the rosary beads. When she sat bolt upright and looked at him, her face glistened with tears. "It's all right, Judy," whispered Forbes, slipping onto one knee to get closer to her. "Don't cry. It'll be all over soon."

"This is all my fault, isn't it?" she sobbed. "You both knew all along, didn't you? You knew."

"Yes, I'm afraid we did."

"That's what all those detentions and lines were for— you were trying to get me out of the way."

Forbes reached out and pressed the back of his hand against Judy's hot, wet cheek. "It's all right, Judy; there's no need to cry about it now. Perhaps we were wrong to keep the truth from you, but yes, we knew."

"When did you guess?"

"Mr Peterson seems to have worked it out during the holidays," said Forbes, letting Judy take his hand in hers. She held his fingers tightly, unable to keep herself from trembling. "He confided in me when he was sure he could trust me, but the problem was evidence. We couldn't risk your piecing it all together before we had a strong enough case."

"And now I've wrecked everything."

Forbes stood up abruptly, troubled by a distant noise. "Don't think about it, Judy. Quiet now."

He closed and locked the door as quickly as he could and had only just sat down again when the door flew open.

There stood Miss Miller, breathless and angry, her eyes blazing with rage. Forbes got to his feet. "Where is she?" she shouted, striding towards him in such a purposeful manner that he stepped back without thinking. It would have looked comical to an outsider; the woman was so short Forbes towered over her, but he found it impossible to stand his ground with those furious hawklike eyes glowering at him.

"Madam, I do not have the pleasure of understanding you," Forbes replied, steeling himself enough to stand still and return her glare. "Are you referring to Judith Randall?"

"You know perfectly well I am referring to her," said Miss Miller. "She's here, isn't she? She never ran away. Even that impudent little thing wouldn't be foolhardy enough to run out into the night without so much as a halfpenny in her pocket."

"Perhaps she went to find Annie," Forbes ventured. He was sure Miss Miller could sense the presence of another person in the room, though he could not for the life of him imagine how. "You know what friends they are."

"A good effort, young man. If Judith had been anywhere near that cottage, Mr Peterson would not have invited me to join him there. I am certain of that."

"He mightn't have known . . ." Forbes trailed off at the sight of Miss Miller marching towards the window and flinging it open. "What are you doing?"

"So, she's not run out this way after all," she commented aloud. "She's so clumsy she would never have jumped clear of those flowerpots without unsettling at least one of them."

"Miss Miller, I'm afraid I do not understand you," Forbes said, stepping between the headmistress and the cupboard. "Why should she have come in here? And why would I be protecting her? The poor girl's been expelled; there is nothing further I can do to help her."

Miss Miller's eyes raked the room for any sign of life before coming to rest on the cupboard door. "The poor girl is very good at inspiring hapless men to protect her. Open that cupboard."

Forbes felt bile rising in his throat. "Why? It's only a storage cupboard. Was there something you needed?"

Miss Miller pushed past him and gave the door handle a yank, but it refused to budge. Forbes offered up a silent prayer that Judy would keep her head and not make a sound to betray her presence there. "Give me the key."

He tried a different tactic. "I'm sorry, but this is preposterous. It's Mr Peterson's cupboard. He keeps his papers in there."

"I need to satisfy my curiosity, that is all. Hand over the key."

"I don't have it. As I said, it's Mr Peterson's cupboard. He always carries the key in his pocket."

Miss Miller shook her head and walked towards Peterson's desk. "I will leave him a note," she said, sifting through a pile of unmarked exercises on his desk for a piece of scrap paper. "Do close those curtains; there's a good chap."

Forbes distracted himself with the task of closing the curtains, hoping against all hope that Peterson would not return at that precise moment. There was no time to think of anything else. He felt a sudden explosive pain across the back of his neck and staggered forward with the force of the missile hitting him. He blacked out before his head hit the ground.

"Couldn't lie to a child," said Elsa to herself as she bent

down and searched his pockets, retrieving the key without difficulty. She threw open the door in one violent movement, glanced down at the girl's white, frightened face and brought her fist down as hard as she could against her cheek, stunning her into silence. "Don't make a sound," she said quietly. "Now you'd better come with me."

The shock of being struck so hard made Judy unnaturally compliant, and she allowed herself to be pulled roughly to her feet, jolting to a stop only when she saw Mr Forbes lying face down on the ground. "O God!" she whimpered, but Miss Miller pulled her clear of the body.

"Never seen a dead body before, have you, girl?" she asked, with a smile that made Judy want to run for cover. "Don't scream."

Miss Miller twisted the girl's arm behind her back, just tightly enough to force her to move forward. She paused at the door to ensure that the corridor was empty before marching Judy around the corner into the concealment of the school chapel. As a Catholic, Judy had never entered the chapel before and felt a panicked sense of being in forbidden territory as the heavy doors shut behind them, plunging them into sudden twilight. She could just make out the rows and rows of pews standing like ranks of enemy soldiers as they walked down the side aisle, passing a mural with big black lettering proclaiming: "Prepare to Meet Thy God."

"What are you doing?" whispered Judy, finding her voice in spite of the pressure on her arm. "Where are you taking me?"

"Somewhere where we will not be disturbed," Miss Miller responded calmly. "This may take a little while."

"What do you want?" But Judy had never had the slightest talent for deception or misdirection, and she could not even try to sound surprised. She knew precisely why Miss Miller was bearing down on her and what she was after; sounding surprised or trying to lie was clearly futile. She doubted it would even buy her time.

"You have stolen something that belongs to me," said Miss Miller, using the tone she would normally have used to explain a basic fact to a brainless child. "Now, be a good girl and give it back; then we may both go about our business without troubling one another again."

A denial froze in Judy's throat. She just couldn't say it. "What did you do to Mr Forbes?"

"Oh, don't try to distract me, girl. Of course he isn't dead. I merely put him to sleep for a little while so that I could deal with you. Now where is my letter?"

The darkness of the room was as stifling as the cupboard. Judy looked about for the friendly face of an angel or the Sacred Heart or Our Lady Help of Christians, but there were blank walls and dark corners everywhere, squeezing the hope out of her. "I don't have a letter."

"You stole a letter from my safe," said Miss Miller. "A very wicked thing, stealing. You're not too young to go to prison. Now, if you give it back to me, I shan't have you arrested."

The threat meant nothing to Judy; she knew Miss Miller would never summon the police to assist her in her treacherous activities. She wondered if Mr Peterson had returned to the staff room and realised what had happened. As soon as he did, he would start looking for her, but she doubted it would occur to him to come in here; the first place he would go would be Miss Miller's study.

"I am waiting, Judy," said Miss Miller, her tone hardening. She had let go of Judy's arm, having no further need to make her move, and was standing before her with her hands on her hips, awaiting a response. "I know you stole it—you were the last person to go anywhere near my study before it disappeared. Now hand it over!"

Judy became aware of a thin line of light forming a narrow arch in the opposite corner. A door to the outside world. If she could only get out of this room, she could use the one natural ability she had and run like the blazes until she reached help or at least until she was far away from her antagonist. "I don't have it!" declared Judy, as loudly as she dared, pushing Miss Miller aside and making a dash for the door. Judy felt the cold, hard metal of the latch beneath her hands, but the door was bolted somewhere and refused to open.

"Need some fresh air, do you?" enquired Miss Miller, appearing behind her. Judy flinched as something heavy jarred against the middle of her spine. She knew what it was without seeing it. "Let's go, shall we?" said Miss Miller amiably. "Away from prying eyes. Just remember, before you do anything idiotic, you can't run faster than a bullet."

~

"What the hell happened?" demanded Peterson, as Forbes blinked bewilderedly at him. Peterson had entered the room after a more successful telephone call to the police, to find Forbes out for the count and the cupboard door swinging on its hinges. He knelt down and proffered a hand, but Forbes planted his hands firmly on the floor and heaved himself drunkenly to his feet.

"The old witch hurled something at me," he said, clutching the back of his neck. It hurt abominably.

"Well, thank God for small mercies that she didn't pick up that glass paperweight instead, or you'd be making your excuses to Saint Peter," snapped Peterson.

Forbes looked blankly at the empty cupboard. "Oh, dear God! She knew, you know. She knew we were hiding her in here." He looked helplessly at Peterson for support. "She won't hurt Judy; she's only a kid." But Peterson was silent. "Do you still have the letter?"

"Naturally."

"She'll realise you have it. It's only a matter of time."

"That's the least of our problems," said Peterson, making for the door. "We have to find them. The police have assured me that they are on their way, but Elsa will hardly hang around waiting for them to turn up. She must know she has very little time."

Forbes hurried after Peterson into the corridor. "Surely it can't be that bad. We'll never find them. It will take hours to search the entire school; there are hundreds of little rooms and alcoves. And that's before we've reached the grounds—"

"Harry, stop prattling!" Peterson hissed, hurrying past the chapel to the base of the back stairs. "It is as bad as it can be. Elsa is a spy on the run. The letter Judy stole from her is evidence enough to see her hang as a traitor. She will do anything she has to in order to retrieve it; her life depends on forcing Judy to give it up."

"But Judy doesn't have it! If she doesn't have it, she's safe."

Peterson clutched his head in his hands as though he had a blinding hangover. "Harry, don't you understand? Judith Randall is going to die tonight. Elsa will keep her alive only long enough to regain possession of the letter she was sent by her Nazi spymasters. Judy is another gem for the prosecution. Even if she hadn't taken a letter written in German from a safe, even if she hadn't witnessed Elsa taking photographs of the coastal defences, she has now been the victim of an abduction. There can be no going back. At the very least, Elsa will have to account for that, and she cannot possibly find herself on trial."

Forbes looked up at the dark stairwell, weighing the usefulness of going that way. He was a teacher, and a teacher on his way to another life; the school had never felt like a prison to him as it must have for so many of the girls because he had always known he could leave. It was the first time he had felt trapped—trapped in the middle of a maze full of dead ends and misdirection. "How long do we have?" Forbes asked.

"Elsa's a fool if she hangs around for more than half an hour, and she's no fool. Poor dear Judy has blown our cover; Elsa knows we're coming for her, and she has almost certainly worked out that the police will follow."

Forbes sat down on the stairs, the mathematician in him taking over in place of panic. "Every problem has a solution," he said to himself.

"No, it doesn't!" Peterson snapped. "Keep your wits about you, please."

But Forbes—who had an extraordinary talent for figures and a hopeless memory for words—remembered just one expression his first maths master had taught him. "In mathematics, every problem has a solution." Of course, Forbes knew now that that was not strictly true, but it calmed his nerves contemplating the idea. "If we have thirty minutes, that gives us time to search two locations—taking into account the time needed to get to them. Four if we split up."

"There are hundreds of possible hiding places around the buildings and outbuildings," said Peterson. "It'll be like finding a needle in a haystack."

"Narrow down the possibilities," said Forbes, his eyes closed with the effort to concentrate. "Remove all the places where there are other people present—the dormitories, the infirmary, the staff lodgings. All the places close to them, all the places that are too obvious—"

"Hurry!" snapped Peterson, but Forbes gestured for him not to interrupt. They were caught in the Minotaur's labyrinth, and only a mathematician's cold logic would show them the way of escape.

~

Judy had never entered the sports pavilion in the dark before, but for a few blissful minutes she felt a sense of relief overtaking her. As soon as they stepped through the door, Miss Miller removed her hand from Judy's hair and Judy felt the metal barrel disappearing from the point in her back where the pressure had become painful. She took advantage of the momentary freedom to step away from her abductor—not to attempt an escape, because she knew it was impossible, but simply to separate herself from the woman's horrible physical presence. She was about to turn and face her when a sudden crack against the side of her head knocked her for six and she was thrown flat on her face onto the springy wooden floor.

They were in the vast equipment cupboard, an area the size of a generous bedroom, hemmed in by the shadows of benches and racks containing javelins and lacrosse sticks, ladders, and ropes hanging against the walls in a mass of coils and knots. Judy could smell that familiar odour of wood polish and oil; it should have reassured her that she was in one of the few places on earth that held no bad memories and nothing to fear, but in her punch-drunk confusion, Judy could not understand why Miss Miller could have brought her to such a place at all.

"You have something that belongs to me," said Miss Miller calmly, placing her foot on Judy's wrist to stop her from rising. "No, don't get up. Just hand over the letter you stole from my safe, and we'll say nothing further about it."

"But I haven't got your letter!" protested Judy. "You can check—" The rest of the sentence was strangled in her throat. Judy found it impossible to breathe or to even cry out as Miss Miller pressed her foot down on her wrist. Judy felt a series of explosions like firecrackers going off inside her arm as the tiny fragile bones began to fracture and snap, before a shrieking, grating noise filled the room. In her panic, Judy was unaware that the sound was coming from deep inside her own body; she saw burning white lights flashing in front of her head and the choking sensation of acid rising up in her throat.

"You have my permission to scream if you really must," Miss Miller assured her, removing her foot to give the girl some breathing space. "No one can hear us in here. Clever, isn't it? Now, here is what we are going to do. You have a letter of mine that is extremely important to me and of no worth to you whatsoever. You will give it back to me or tell me truthfully where you have hidden it. I will take back what is mine and leave you alone."

Judy could feel the ground rolling beneath her as though she were on a ship in stormy seas. She braced herself, waiting for the pain to subside, but even keeping absolutely still had no effect. She was not on a ship at all; she was slipping underwater, her head slipping into the chill darkness . . . A sharp slap in the face made her jump, but in the state she was in, it had little effect. "For goodness' sake, breathe!" Miss Miller commanded. "I'll not have you throwing a faint. Just answer the question!"

"I haven't got it," whispered Judy, but she was still drowning. Her body was drenched with sweat; she could feel the fibres of her blouse sticking to her back as she lay on the floor, and in her confusion, she did not know whether pain or fear was the cause. "Please, I haven't got a letter."

"Then where did you put it?" asked Miss Miller. "Or do I need to break your other wrist to get the answer I need?"

Judy knew she should give an answer, any answer at all that was plausible enough to make her tormentor leave her alone. She ought to claim she had hidden it somewhere awkward to send Miss Miller on a wild-goose chase until the police arrived, but Judy was a hopeless liar at the best of times, and Miss Miller knew it. In a state of blind panic, it was impossible for her to formulate a story, and it took every scrap of strength to stop herself from shouting out Mr Peterson's name.

"Let me ask you another question then," continued Miss

Miller, planting the pointed heel of her shoe on the shoulder of the arm with the broken wrist. "Whom did you give it to? You gave it to someone else, didn't you?"

It may have been a coincidence, or Miss Miller might have known just what she was doing, but the hard point of her heel came down in exactly the place where delicate ligaments crossed, causing a sensation like a powerful electric shock to surge across Judy's neck. She opened her mouth to scream, but the invisible hand was crushing her throat, and her only sound was a faltering moan. All Judy knew was that she would never find a way out of the mess she had got herself into and that it was all her fault. She had blundered into a situation that had never been any of her business, and if she could not keep her mouth shut, somebody other than her was going to pay.

Judy felt herself sliding along a tunnel, the pain rising and falling as she slipped in and out of consciousness. She was forced onto her back, jolting her wrist, but despair was taking over from fear, and she could not find the energy to scream again. "Mr Forbes or Mr Peterson?" came the next question. "Or have you done something unpredictable for the first time in your life?"

"Elsa!"

There was an excruciating silence as the two women took in the presence of intruders. "*Goeienaand*, Elsa," said the voice from the door. "*Ek is verlore.*"

The effect on Miss Miller was immediate. Judy felt the woman's hands trembling a second before she staggered back, turning to face the man who had spoken to her in a mysterious language no one else understood. Elsa looked up at John Peterson, but an answer refused to come. "It's been so long since I've spoken my mother tongue," she said faintly. "I can't seem to find the words."

Peterson took a cautious step towards her, but she remembered herself and snatched up the pistol she had carelessly put down, seconds before he could reach it. "Let her alone," said Peterson in English. "I have the letter, but it's useless to you now. The police will be here at any moment, and they know everything."

"You're lying," said Elsa quickly. "I would have heard the engines."

"Not from this side of the building you wouldn't." Peterson attempted another step, but Elsa grabbed Judy by the neck, forcing her up onto her knees. "Don't do this, Elsa. Whatever quarrel you have with the English, it is not her fault."

"It is her fault that she interfered!" shouted Elsa. "It's her fault that she couldn't mind her own business! What right had she to meddle?"

"Elsa, she is hardly more than a child." Peterson watched helplessly as Elsa pressed the barrel of the pistol against Judy's temple. If Elsa had been merely angry with the girl, he might have found some way to calm her down; but she was possessed by the terror of a cornered animal, and Peterson had no way of knowing how she would respond. "Please, Elsa, put the gun down. You're not going to hang for a murder you don't even want to commit."

"I'll hang anyway," Elsa choked out. "They'll kill me as they killed everyone I loved. They showed no mercy during that war, and they'll show none now."

"Put the gun down, Elsa."

The three of them flinched at the sound of many pairs of footsteps approaching the door; the flicker of torches pierced through the windows. "Step outside and tell them I've taken a hostage. I'll kill her if they attempt to arrest me."

Peterson looked Judy in the eye; she was on her knees, her lower arm hanging in a painfully unnatural position, her head forced to one side by the pressure of the gun, which now rested against her jugular. Now that it came to it, Peterson could not bring himself to believe that Elsa would go through with it, actually pull the trigger, even if she had been commanded to do so. It was one thing to believe that a human being's life was worthless; it was quite another to turn such a thought into action by despatching a person who was in the way. Nevertheless, Peterson had seen fear and retribution at work before, he had seen reprisals carried out by those he would never have thought capable. He shuffled backwards in the direction of the door, not daring to take his eyes off Elsa and Judy until his hand touched the door handle and he was forced to turn to nudge it open and step through. He felt the cool of the outside air touching him but in his nervous state, it had no soothing effect on him. Peterson was standing before three constables and an older man he took to be the sergeant, all standing in readiness to burst in.

"She's armed and she's taken a hostage, a girl from the school," said Peterson as calmly as possible. "She says she'll shoot her if you attempt to arrest her. Please stay well back."

"You can't go back in there, sir," said the sergeant, stepping forward. "It's too dangerous for a civilian."

"I have no choice," said Peterson. "I'm the only one

either of them trusts, and I can't leave Judy alone. She's injured and scared. They're both scared."

Peterson pushed open the door, hesitating in the doorway with his hands raised above his head to ensure that Elsa knew he was still unarmed. Very slowly, he stepped back into the room, letting the door shut softly behind him. Judy was still on her knees, her face deathly white against the black curls that clung to her forehead and neck in damp swirls. Elsa had not moved either, and Peterson noticed her gun hand trembling. He had not witnessed an injured person in such immediate danger since he had been put on a ship to England all those years before. He had not found himself so close to a gun . . . Peterson felt his chest tightening and that paralysing sensation of his breath being knocked out of his body again.

There were wire fences everywhere, the perimeters of a giant cage, and a frail woman shivering with an infernal fever that was slowly draining her energies. In the blink of an eye, his most terrible memory engulfed him, threatening to take him down. He fixed his gaze on Judy's desperate figure. She was not frail or thin like his mother had been, starved by the long months in the camp and ravaged by cholera, but she was gasping and panting for breath with the desperation of a person who knows each breath might be his last. It was that desperation he remembered so vividly, that sense of death closing in around a person too petrified to fight it anymore.

"Come on now, Elsa," said Peterson gently, reaching out a hand to her. "Put the gun down. Your family wouldn't have wanted this."

"How can you say that?" demanded Elsa. "My mother begged me to avenge her death. I'm doing precisely what they would have wanted."

"Elsa, Judy wasn't even born when you and your family were sent to the camps. She knows nothing about what happened to the Boers."

"This is not about her; she just happened to get in the way!" Elsa looked at Peterson in accusation. "All I have ever desired is to bring the British to their knees. I want to see this godforsaken nation utterly destroyed, and I don't care who destroys it."

Peterson swallowed hard, but his mouth was dry. There she was again: a woman so tiny that, even before she had been broken by the war, the farmhands had carried her on their shoulders as though she were a child, laughing at her mock indignation. A woman small enough to fit into the arms of a ten-year-old boy . . . "Elsa, I remember those concentration camps. My mother died in my arms. The guards had to drag her body away by force because I wouldn't let go. But she begged me to forgive. She would have wanted me to be merciful to my enemies."

Elsa's face darkened immediately. A sneer crept over her face, so terrible that Peterson knew he had failed, a split second before he heard the resounding crack of the pistol hitting Judy's head. He darted forwards instinctively, but Elsa was quicker and had the barrel of the gun pressing against the girl's neck again before he could reach her. "Think very carefully before you open your mouth again," whispered Elsa. "It's far too late in the day to start remonstrating with me. You and your kind have already lost. It's only a matter of time."

Peterson searched Judy's face for any signs of life. She was opening her eyes and groaning with pain, momentarily unaware of where she was. He doubted she had been knocked unconscious, but the force of the blow had been enough to stun her into confusion, and she started struggling. "Judy, stay still!" ordered Peterson. "It's all right; just don't move." He could hear the sound of the door opening behind him and knew that the police were running out of patience. "Elsa, if the Nazis take over the country, there will be misery and carnage greater than anything either of us has ever known. There will be concentration camps, there will be public hangings, there will be blood on the streets. Is that what you truly want? Is that the world in which you want these girls to grow up?"

Elsa's eyes rested coldly on Peterson's. "You really don't understand, do you?" she asked with a tone of quiet malice Peterson had heard before. "You ridiculous man, I don't care. All I have ever sought was revenge. I was never going to have to live with the consequences. Now——"

The clatter of a window being thrown open was not loud, but in the condition they were all in, it sounded like a grenade going off, and they were all startled. A squeal left Judy's mouth, but not because of the noise. A tearful Annie had climbed into the pavilion, wrecking her entrance by tumbling forward as she landed.

"Annie, what on earth are you doing?" demanded Peterson. Of all the people he had expected to attempt a rescue, it was not his daughter. "Get out now! Leave!"

"Annie dear, you must go," said Elsa gently, looking up at Annie in something like embarrassment. Peterson felt his blood running cold; she was coaxing her into leaving as though Annie were a little girl who had burst into a dinner party long after her bedtime. Elsa had known Annie would come. "Please go, Annie. This is nothing to do with you."

Annie's eyes were fixed on Elsa; she was avoiding looking directly at Judy, but she was clearly overcome by the sight of her, and Peterson knew better than anyone else that his daughter would never be able to cope with the shock. "Please stop hurting her. This is all my fault!" she protested. "You promised so faithfully you'd protect her. I never would have done it—"

"I meant to protect her!" answered Elsa, and she was almost pleading. "I wanted her out of my school. But a creature like this cannot be protected. Please go. You must go."

But Annie could not move. Her eyes moved desperately from her father to Elsa, as though unsure as to who was the greater threat to her. She focused on Judy, her fists clenched behind her back with the effort. "I'm sorry," she murmured. "I'm so sorry. Please . . ."

Peterson stepped gingerly forward with the intention of encouraging Annie to walk away, but Elsa glared at him, motioning for him to step back. "You will both step back," she said. "Right back to the door, if you don't mind."

"Elsa . . . ," Peterson began.

"Quickly now, I shan't be asking anything else of you." Peterson gestured for Annie to leave the room. She took a last look at Judy as though taking leave of her old friend, and for a moment, it looked as though she would refuse to be parted from her. Then the self-preservation instinct took over, and she hurried out into the arms of the waiting policemen. "There, you see," said Elsa quietly, "Annie's perfectly safe. She was always safe." She paused for a response, but Peterson stared at her in silence. With a massive effort, he forced himself to take three steps back, not daring to take his eyes off Judy and Elsa for a single second. "Thank you," said Elsa, as though she were concluding a staff meeting. She released her grip on Judy, allowing her to slip forward and curl up on the floor, too exhausted to care that the woman was still holding a loaded weapon over her.

"Please . . . ," Judy began, but there was nothing left for her to say.

"Enjoy the respite while you can," Elsa told Judy. She set the gun down and Peterson saw her fiddling with a necklace around her neck that he had somehow failed to notice before then. "The Nazis are coming, and they'll know whom to hang."

A moment later, the room descended into chaos. Elsa slipped a pill into her mouth. Judy lay helplessly on the floor, watching as Peterson rushed forwards, shouting at the top of his voice for Elsa not to do it, when she was already frothing at the mouth and there was a smell of almonds everywhere; there were policemen in their black uniforms and helmets tearing through the room; and lights, after such a long darkness, there were burning lights all around. In the midst of the mayhem that Judy had somehow managed to create, she heard herself crying out for it all to stop . . . she shouted at the top of her voice, not out of pain or panic any longer, but because the world was ending all around her and she had no fight left in her. She was a child screaming because she was afraid of the dark, afraid of monsters prowling in the night, afraid to leave the nursery, not because she expected anyone to put things right, but because the world was ending . . .'

Someone was holding her in his arms, desperately trying to calm her down. "It's all right, Judy, it's all right. Don't look. Please don't look." It was Mr Forbes, lifting her off the ground, out of the way of the swarm of people gathering

164

around Elsa Miller's body. Judy looked back like Lot's wife as she was carried out of the room: Elsa was almost hidden from view, but Judy could make out a hand, white and bony against the wooden floor, the fingers still curled into a fist.

11

A pale, pinched face stared morosely out of the cottage window. She was so drawn from lack of sleep that there was something spectral about her normally hearty looks, and a casual bystander might not have even recognised her as she watched the garden path for any sign of an approaching policeman. A moment later, she disappeared from view, called away from the glass panes by her mother, but she had spent much of the morning keeping watch at the window with her mother desperately trying to draw her away.

"Annie dear, he won't come any more quickly if you stand there waiting for him," said Mary, from the other side of the kitchen. "Please come away. Sit down, and I'll bring you a glass of milk."

Annie hovered by the table, unwilling or unable to settle herself. "Are you sure I oughtn't to pack a bag?" she asked.

Mary went over to her daughter and almost pushed her into the chair. "You are not going to be arrested, dear; they haven't even asked you to present yourself at the police station. Inspector Brennan said it would be acceptable to talk to you in the privacy of your own home. The police simply need to know exactly what happened." Mary went over to the stove to pick up the kettle. "You know, Annie, you needn't have insisted your father leave the house. You mustn't be ashamed; it was her fault, not yours. She lied to you."

Annie nestled her head in her arms. "I thought he was going to die last night; I thought Judy was going to die," she said. "I know he's disappointed in me, even though he promises he isn't. I know *you're* ashamed of me. Why shouldn't you be?"

Mary dropped the kettle into the sink and dashed over to Annie's side. "You mustn't think that!" she insisted. "We were sad, that's all. I suppose I wish you had told me what was going on, and I could have helped you." She pulled a chair closer to her daughter so that she could put an arm around her shoulder, but Annie turned away. "Don't, please don't do that. We need to pull together now. All of us. We need—" A sudden, thunderous rap on the door was greeted by a whimper of panic from Annie, and Mary lost her train of thought. She helped Annie to her feet. "I'll open the door," she said. "You go into the sitting room and settle yourself. Remember, all you have to do is to tell the inspector the truth."

Annie hurried into the sitting room as her mother went to answer the door. Entering the sitting room at all at this time of the day felt unnatural. It was an adult room of polished surfaces and formal, un-lived-in furnishings. Mother's auntie's watercolours hung on the walls; her father's books lined the mahogany bookcases, great heavy tomes with gold leaf edges, written in English, French, German, and even a few other languages Annie didn't recognise. The Petersons were all much happier in the warmth of the kitchen, and that was where they preferred to sit and talk, but her mother would never have shown a stranger into her kitchen. Annie hesitated like Goldilocks in the middle of the room before selecting the high-backed chair nearest the door, on the grounds that it might encourage her to sit up straight. When she sat down and ran her fingers through her hair, she realised she had not even combed and tied her hair back that morning; she had been too sleepily distracted after a night of tears and many hours of tossing and turning. The events of the evening before had played themselves out in her mind over and over again, complicated by her mind desperately imagining how differently she could have done things. In that semiconscious trance created by exhaustion, Annie imagined herself rejecting Miss Miller's overtures, telling her parents everything, doing the sensible thing. She imagined herself in that sports pavilion doing something daring like the heroine of an adventure story; she saw herself overpowering Miss Miller and rescuing her friend, stoically standing where she was, refusing to leave her father's side when she had been instructed to leave. In the misery of the sleepless early morning, she willed herself to have been something other than a gullible, frightened little girl, running to safety whilst two of the people she most loved in the whole world were in mortal danger.

Annie stood up automatically at the sound of voices just outside the door. She would have to come quietly, like a proper grown-up. No fuss, no histrionics. Mother had promised she would not be arrested, but parents had a tendency to tell little fibs like that to avoid a scene, and Annie could not avoid the possibility that she might be marched unceremoniously into the back of a black Humber in a few minutes' time. Annie wondered if the bobby really would put her in handcuffs, but she had never seen a person arrested before, and the only time she had seen a depiction of an arrest in a film had been when she had sloped off to the pictures on holiday and seen a Jimmy Cagney film. *We've got the place surrounded!* Now that she thought about it, she hadn't told her parents about that outing either.

The door opened, and a grey-haired man who looked old enough to be her grandfather stepped into the room. Annie looked at him in bewilderment. "Are you a policeman?" she asked doubtfully. "You're not in uniform. I thought you'd have a helmet and a truncheon." *I thought you'd be about my father's age*, she thought, but Annie was far too well mannered to say anything about that.

The old man smiled kindly. "I am a policeman, but it has been many years since I was last in uniform. My name is Detective Inspector Brennan. You must be Anne." Annie nodded. "Good. I think you'd better sit down. I'm afraid I need to ask you some questions."

"I know," she said, taking the cue to settle herself back down in her chair. Annie watched as he sat opposite her and took some papers out of his bag, placing them tidily on the table in front of him. It seemed to take an age for him to get his fountain pen out of its little leather box; his movements were painfully slow and deliberate, as though he were loading a gun. "What's going to happen to me?" she blurted out, unable to wait anymore.

Inspector Brennan was now taking his time removing a bulging rectangular pouch from his breast pocket, the edge of a pair of reading glasses slightly protruding. Annie might have been forgiven for thinking he was deliberately tormenting her, but she suspected that he was like all official people: terribly particular about absolutely everything. She focused her attention on the embroidered flowers inexpertly covering the inspector's glasses case. It had obviously been made for him by a child, perhaps a granddaughter. Annie tried desperately to imagine the inspector sitting on the floor beside a vast Christmas tree with an adorable little child in pigtails presenting him with a small rectangular package. It did not work. Even in the midst of a Christmas idyll, Annie still saw him suited and booted, scrutinising the doll-like granddaughter for signs that she had breached the law.

The moment the inspector had put on his reading glasses, he looked up at Annie over the half-moon lenses and smiled again. "Well, my dear, you might be in a whole lot of trouble. Aiding and abetting a traitor in time of war is a very serious matter."

"I thought I was helping my headmistress!" Annie began, but she could feel herself welling up already and knew this was not a good start. "She promised so faithfully that everything would be all right!"

"It's all right," he put in quickly. "Please do not alarm yourself. Your parents have already told me that you are a good girl who has never been in trouble before about anything. I would like to help you, but I will need your cooperation. Do you understand?"

Annie nodded again. This was not at all what she had expected. For some reason, she had had visions of a desperately sinister interrogation in a bare, windowless room, probably a scene she had gleaned from a film she was never supposed to watch. Instead, here she was, sitting in an armchair in her own sitting room, in the presence of a man with the manner of an old country doctor, who was giving every impression of being on her side. She felt an overwhelming urge to confess everything to him, the way she might have felt the need to make a clean breast of it in the confessional, knowing that after an Act of Contrition and absolution, everything would be all right again. It did not occur to her that he might be deliberately doing a "good cop" impression to win her over, having noted immediately that it would be the easiest way to get answers out of her. "I'll tell you everything," she promised fervently. "What do you need to know?"

"That's the ticket," he said, starting to write. The scratching noise of the silver nib chafing against paper sounded absurdly loud in the quiet room. "Perhaps you could start by telling me what she told you. What did Miss Miller tell you she was doing?"

"Would you mind if I close my eyes?" asked Annie. She needed to tell her story in darkness, as though she were really in the confessional and could not see the face of the priest. "Please?"

Inspector Brennan cleared his throat, in what she suspected was an attempt to stop himself from laughing. "If you wish."

Annie duly covered her eyes. There, that was much easier. "She said she was trying to stop people from dying. She said that wars were terrible things and that if Britain didn't make peace with Germany, then thousands, perhaps millions, of people here would die. She said the Germans were coming, that they were already conquering Europe, and England would be next. The case was hopeless, but Churchill was too stubborn to make peace; he would insist we fight until everyone was dead. She said she wasn't a traitor—" Annie covered her face with one hand. She had to open her eyes because tears were unexpectedly forcing their way through, and she did not want him to see. She wished now that she had slept better. "She said she was giving information to the Germans so that there would *have* to be peace. It was the kindest thing to do, like—like, well, taking one's little brother's catapult away so that he can't fight anymore. I think that's what she said. I'm sorry . . ."

Annie was aware of her mother's presence next to her. "Annie, please keep going. Just tell the inspector everything."

Annie shook her head. "I'm sorry. I'm not sure I'm even saying everything right. I'm afraid I didn't really understand her at all when she was explaining everything. I've never much understood this sort of thing, but it all sounded frightfully sensible. Everything Miss Miller said sounded sensible."

"I understand," reassured the inspector. "Tell me what you remember, even if it doesn't appear to make much sense. Do you remember her telling you anything else?"

Annie looked directly at him. She was surprised he was not shocked or angry, but his calm, steady gaze did not waver. It was strange, but part of her wanted him to know everything, as though he could help her make sense of it all. "Yes, she talked a lot. I . . . I realised afterwards she made me a form captain only so that she would have a reason to talk to me in private. She said lots of things. To start with, it sounded sensible. She wanted to stop all those people from dying, even if it meant helping the Germans. But then she started to say other things, that the country was a mess anyway."

"Indeed?"

"Yes." Annie noticed the inspector sitting up and leaning a little closer to her, evidently interested. She needed no further encouragement than the full, sincere attention of an older person. "She said the country had lost its way, and I wasn't to listen to the things people were saying about Hitler. He'd done marvellous things for Germany. The country had gone to pot, but he had sorted it out. It was just that not everybody likes change, of course, and people were in the way but didn't know it. Some people didn't belong."

"Like your friend?"

Annie could feel herself breaking again; she felt her mother placing a clean, starched white handkerchief in her hand, and she accepted it more for the distraction than anything else. "She said if I did what she wanted, she would look after Judy. She would make sure nothing bad happened to her. Every time I didn't want to do what she wanted, she'd tell me that if we didn't work together, they would take her away and I'd never see her again."

Inspector Brennan looked at Mary, who had turned her face away from him sharply. They both knew that what Annie was describing was a condensed version of the rhetoric that had poisoned an entire nation. Poison was best administered very slowly, drip by venomous drip, from an authority figure that an impressionable young mind would instinctively trust. It was the process millions of young Germans had experienced in much more powerful form, and they had few opportunities for quarantine. Unlike Annie. "Mrs Peterson," said the inspector calmly, "I think your daughter needs a cup of tea, don't you? Don't worry, she'll be perfectly all right with me."

Mary looked at Annie, who nodded in agreement, and Mary reluctantly fled the room. The inspector waited until Mary had closed the door behind her before turning his attention back to Annie. "There's something you are not telling me," he said quietly, "perhaps something you didn't want to say in front of your mother. What is it?"

Annie glanced anxiously at the closed door before speaking rapidly. "Please don't tell my mother! She'll be dreadfully upset!"

"I shan't tell her anything if I do not have to," promised Inspector Brennan. "You'd better be quick in case she comes back."

"It wasn't just Judy who Miss Miller said had no place in the world anymore," said Annie, at the same quick pace. "It was my father. She said he was so old-fashioned, so out of place—always in church, counting his beads on his knees, the sort of person who could never change. She said that without help, without someone to protect him, he would get into terrible trouble. They would put him in prison. They might even—well, she said it would be such a pity, that he was such a fine man, but one could not stand in the way of progress, and he didn't understand."

Inspector Brennan wrote down some notes before replacing the lid of his fountain pen and removing his glasses, signalling that the first part of the interview was over. "You must have been desperately confused," he said gently. "Did you not think to tell anyone? You have kind parents, a loyal friend. There must have been someone in whom you could have confided?"

Annie shook her head vigorously. "She told me over and over again that if I told anyone, it would be a disaster. She would be arrested, and there would be no one to protect me or Judy or my family when the Germans came. Then when she started making me do bad things, she said that if the police found out, they would hang me." *Let it end here*, she

175

thought miserably. *Let him tell me I've said enough.* She heard the creak of the door opening and her mother walking in with a tea tray.

Mary put the tray down between Annie and Inspector Brennan, pouring the tea with undue care. The silence in the room was excruciating. "Would you rather I made myself scarce?" Mary offered, standing up straight. She had not poured a cup of tea for herself. "I quite understand if it's easier."

"It's entirely up to you," said Inspector Brennan to Annie. "It is of no consequence to me either way. However, for what it's worth, I cannot help thinking that keeping secrets from your parents has only done you harm. In my experience, it almost invariably does more harm than good."

Annie looked up at her mother. She could feel herself blushing with shame. "Well . . ."

"I'll go if you want me to," said Mary quickly, reaching out to give Annie's hand a squeeze. "No one likes to own up in front of her mother. I'm not here to make life more difficult for you."

Mary drew her hand away, but Annie seized hold of it on impulse. "Please stay," she said. "I shall feel so much better afterwards if I don't have to talk about it ever again."

Mary smiled and stepped back until she was standing behind Annie, well away from her field of vision. "Why don't I stay where you can't see me?" she volunteered. "Then you can forget I'm listening."

Annie looked back at the inspector, who had discreetly put down his teacup and picked up his pen. "Well, I suppose, to start with, it was fetching and carrying," said Annie. "In fact, it was almost always fetching and carrying. I like running, and I have a bicycle. She said nobody would suspect a girl going up and down to the woods—and of course, I have more freedom to move around."

"The girls are not allowed out-of-bounds without permission," Mary explained. "It would have aroused too much suspicion if she had conscripted one of the other girls. They are watched more closely. Annie was perfect because she lives on the school site but she is not a boarder. I quite often send her into the village on errands myself."

"What sort of things did she give you?"

"Letters mostly, messages. But sometimes heavier packages that I had to put in my basket under a cloth."

"Did you ever look inside to see what she was giving you?" he asked.

Annie shook her head vigorously. "Of course not. It would have been sneaky reading other people's letters. She would have known anyhow; the envelopes and parcels were always sealed."

Inspector Brennan leaned forward, sensing a way in. "Come now, an inquisitive girl like you must have been tempted to find out what was going on."

"I wanted to do the right thing!" exclaimed Annie, genuinely insulted that he imagined her to be a nosy parker. "She trusted me!"

The inspector sighed, refusing to give up. "What about the person to whom you gave the messages? Did you meet him?"

Annie shook her head. "No, Miss Miller said it was safer for me that way. There was a place in the woods, an old bird box not too far from the path. I was supposed to leave things there and go away immediately."

"You never lingered? Never waited to see who came?"

And answer came there none. Brennan looked at Annie's bowed head and sighed. The girl was the perfect accomplice: loyal to a fault, and credulous enough to believe anything she was told and to do as she was told if the person issuing the orders carried enough authority. In another country, it would already be too late to help her, the good girl skilfully moulded into an obedient retainer until she no longer remembered the person she had once been. "I'm very sorry, sir," came a plaintive voice, breaking into his thoughts. "I'm sorry about the telephone lines. I'm sorry about the photographs."

"So it was you who cut the lines," he said without emotion. "Another case closed."

"But that was months ago!" exclaimed Mary. "How long has this been going on?"

"I'm sorry," murmured Annie. "They fixed them again quite quickly, if it helps." She knew it didn't. *Nothing* could help.

"They had to fix them quickly," Inspector Brennan explained, and there was only the mildest edge to his voice to signal he was becoming impatient. "Cutting wires does not just cause a great deal of inconvenience to a great many people; if there were an invasion, the breakdown in communication could be disastrous." Annie did not stir. "I daresay you didn't know that, though, did you?"

"Oh yes, I did," answered Annie, completely failing to notice that he was trying to protect her. "She said it was just practising for the real thing." She looked round and saw her mother with her head in her hands. "Sorry."

Sorry. A girl very comfortably at the age of reason who was perfectly capable of discerning the difference between right and wrong had made a decision that was illegal and immoral, but she was sorry. She was so *sorry*. The inspector looked sternly at her. "Anne, I don't want to be too hard on you because you have clearly been misled by a person you should have been able to trust, but boys not much older than you are dying for their country as we speak. You're not a baby; you must have known how serious it was to do such a thing. Never mind an invasion—what if someone were in urgent need of help? A man struck down by a sudden illness or accident who needed a doctor? A fire even?"

Annie's mouth opened and shut, but she could think of nothing else to say other than to repeat her apology. The word "sorry" sounded a little inadequate now. She shook her head and stared down at her hands, willing herself away from the room.

"It was you whom Judy saw taking photographs of the coastal defences, wasn't it?" demanded Mary, taking advantage of the silence. "It wasn't Miss Miller after all."

"She said it was better if I did it," Annie explained, but she felt so drained by the increasingly hostile atmosphere that her only desire was for the whole conversation to come to an end. "Miss Miller said I was more agile and that if I were caught, I would only get a telling off for wandering under the wire. I was to tell them that photography was my hobby. No one would suspect me, but they would suspect her if she were found out there."

Mary gave up on any pretence at keeping her distance and sat down at the table between Annie and Inspector Brennan.

179

"Did Judy really not realise it was you?" she asked. "She was convinced it was Miss Miller. Even from a distance with your back to her, your stature is so different."

Annie turned her head away from the inspector, leaving him to feel as though he were eavesdropping on a domestic conversation. "I think the poor thing told herself it had to be Miss Miller. It wouldn't have occurred to her that I could have anything to do with all this—she thought I was too boring. She wanted it to be Miss Miller; she didn't want it to be me. So it wasn't me she saw."

Mary slipped her hands over her face. "I can't help thinking that when Miss Miller expelled Judy, she might have wanted her out of the way immediately because she realised she could implicate both of you. I mean, if Judy was observing you taking those photographs, not Miss Miller, then Miss Miller may well have been watching you. She might have thought that Judy had realised you were involved and might start pestering you for answers. You might have ended up saying something indiscreet."

Annie jumped to her feet, almost tripping over her own shoelaces in the process. "But I never meant to hurt her! I didn't want her to be expelled! I never told her to throw ink all over Ursy! I didn't want her to get expelled the other time either—Miss Miller didn't tell me why I had to put the cashbox in Judy's locker!"

"Annie, sit down," said Mary gently, ignoring the latest bombshell Annie had dropped. Another uncertainty cleared up. "No one was blaming you for getting Judy expelled; I'm simply trying to put the pieces together." Mary resisted the urge to draw Annie into her arms; there was something so

180

endearingly childish about her indignation at being accused of causing her friend to be expelled, when the girl had come within a whisker of being shot dead. Mary looked instead at the inspector. "I suppose you will have to search for the man now, Inspector," she asked, "now that you know that Annie was passing messages to a third party?"

Inspector Brennan shook his head. "I'm afraid that's unlikely. Chances are, the man concerned fled as soon as he heard about the rumpus at the school. With so many men moving about the country, being called up, it won't be at all easy to trace one run away. We don't have anything to go on." He waited until Annie stopped whimpering. "Is there anything else you need to tell me, my dear?"

Annie shook her head. "I'm sorry. Will Judy be all right?"

The inspector gathered together his things. "Your father has gone to see her in hospital, and I suspect she will make a full recovery. Thank you for your assistance in my enquiries."

Annie rose to her feet. "I'm not going to be arrested then?"

Inspector Brennan nodded to Mary as though sharing a private joke. "I'm not sure we have room for you; both our cells are occupied this morning." He moved to the door. "There was one more thing—though you needn't answer if you'd rather not."

"Yes, Inspector?"

"Did you do what Miss Miller wanted simply out of loyalty, or did a small part of you like what she told you?"

Annie lowered her head, praying that this was the last agony he was going to put her through. "It's like I said—

it all sounded so sensible, and it was a lark to be part of something so new and powerful. But since you ask, no. I don't think I should like to live in a world without Judy."

"Or your father?"

"Or my father. I hope that counts for something."

Inspector Brennan patted her shoulder, waiting while she plucked up the courage to look at him. "It counts for a great deal. You need to take a good, hard look at your actions over the past few months. Then, if I were you, I'd use your considerable energy and sense of loyalty serving the war effort. There are many ways to atone for what you have done and it doesn't pay to brood over one's mistakes."

Annie watched as her mother led the inspector out of the room. She waited—frozen to the spot—until she heard the front door open and close. Loneliness was not a concept she had ever understood, but standing alone in the one room of the house where she felt unwelcome, Annie felt the horror of isolation. Tears came, but there were always going to be tears with so many emotions crashing around inside her— shame, grief, an overwhelming sense of relief that everything was out in the open now. That was the trouble with a secret: it always began with a sense of excitement and subterfuge, holding so much promise; almost imperceptibly, the secret took on a life of its own as a conspirator and a thief, manipulating close confidences, stealing happy moments, dragging the recipient into the hinterland of self-isolation where the most important words could never be spoken and no friend or loved one could trespass. And all this whilst outwardly nothing appeared to have changed.

Annie's mother found her, several minutes later, curled up on the rug like a small animal. Mary stood by the door in case her footsteps might startle her. "The inspector's left now, Annie," she said gently. "He has assured me that he will not come back. Your name will not appear in any of the records. In the eyes of the law, you were never involved." She paused, hoping that Annie would lift her head or at least acknowledge her in some way, but she did not move. "Annie dear, this never happened. As far as I'm concerned and your father is concerned, this whole episode can be forgotten. We will never speak of it again."

Annie raised her head very slowly. "I shan't be able to look at any of you again!" she wailed. "Even if you don't speak of it, I know you'll be thinking about it. It's the same thing!"

Mary stepped a little closer to her and sat down on the edge of the rug. "Annie, when I said it would be forgotten, I meant it. Remember what the inspector said about not brooding over past mistakes? Well, it does no good to brood over other people's mistakes either. None of us wants to rake over what's happened. We can all let it go."

Annie slipped miserably back down onto the rug until the side of her head was pressing against the soft green-and-red fibres. "Do you promise?" she asked. "Properly promise?"

The tone and choice of words was so reminiscent of the playground that Mary half-wondered whether she was expected to answer "Cross my heart and hope to die!" Instead, she repeated: "Annie, we all have moments in our lives we wish we could wipe away. It's part of being an adult."

"I don't know what to say to Dad when he gets home!" Annie blurted out. "I hid in my room this morning, pretending to be asleep until after he'd left."

Mary stood up, tapping Annie on the shoulder as she did

so. "Come on, get up. Up off the floor now." She watched as Annie reluctantly heaved herself to her feet, resisting the urge to assist her. Even standing up, Annie managed to avoid looking at her mother, and Mary found herself addressing Annie's unkempt head, which reminded her unfortunately of a small bale of hay. "Annie, I can't pretend that I wasn't shocked by what you told the inspector, but no one is angry with you, least of all your father. If either of us feels anything, I suppose we're a little sorry to think that we didn't know what was happening to you all this time. It's hard to think of that woman poisoning your mind and blackmailing you into helping her whilst all along we had no idea."

"I would have told you . . . ," Annie began, but it seemed so pointless to say it now. "I'm just glad I don't have to pretend anymore."

Annie made her way to the door. "It's good to have you back," said Mary, following her out of the room. "That's all that matters."

"Thank you." Annie paused on the stairs. "Do you suppose I might have a bath? Will there be enough hot water?"

Mary smiled at the sudden incursion of the domestic into what was probably the most serious conversation the two of them had ever had. "I'll boil some water now. Why don't you go up and get ready? There's some lavender oil in my cabinet."

Mary watched as Annie walked slowly upstairs. It already seemed a long time since she had been in the habit of running up and down those steep steps, taking them two or three at a time, but Mary had not noticed the change at the time. It was all unravelling, the home she had so carefully nurtured and served for so many years. Her youngest child was very nearly a woman, and the war would carry her far away from her. A few years ago, she might never have left, following the well-worn path from pupil to teacher that Mary herself had trod so blithely long ago, but she was not so naive as to imagine it would be the same for her daughter. An act of severance was taking place between nations, between peoples, between families; husbands were being parted from wives, sons from parents, daughters too. No one would be spared this act of uprooting and scattering. Mary could only pray that—if God were good to them all—they might all survive the years of violence to come and, somehow or other, find their way home again through the darkness.

12

It was after two in the afternoon before Judy awoke from her drug-induced sleep. She opened her eyes and immediately found herself in a room that was spinning round and round, threatening to throw her into oblivion. There was something smooth and hard wrapped tightly around her arm, weighing it down, and a dull, thudding pain crept across her temple like a pulse reminding her that she was at least still alive. The fingers of her free hand went up to her head, touching the soft fibres of what felt like a dressing covering a painful, raised area near her hairline.

"Matron?" she called, but her throat was dry and papery. She thought she must be in the school infirmary. There was that familiar smell of carbolic soap and starch. A woman in uniform, her head primly covered, stood nearby. "Matron?"

"It's quite all right, my dear," came a kindly response that was not Matron's. "You are recovering in hospital. You are quite safe." Judy looked blankly at the woman, who was thinner and older than Matron but had the same calm, matter-of-fact manner. "I shall inform the doctor that you are awake."

Judy watched the woman leave the room with a swish of skirts and glanced helplessly around her. Of course, she was not in the school infirmary; she was in a small room with no other beds or sick girls to contend with. The only

187

connection with school was Mr Peterson, who was sitting like a night watchman in an easy chair by the window. "Hello, Judy," he said quietly, standing up and approaching her bedside. "How are you feeling?"

The sight of Mr Peterson's haggard, unshaven face brought her back to earth with a jolt, and she closed her eyes, a split second too late to stop tears sliding sideways into her hair. "I'm so sorry," she said, her eyes still tightly closed. "Mr Forbes told me everything."

Mr Peterson placed a hand on her arm. "It's all right, Judy; don't upset yourself. I'm afraid we went about it all wrong. We should have known you would never give up once you were on the scent, but until there was enough evidence, we couldn't expose her."

"I'm so stupid."

"On the contrary, Judy, you are a little too clever for your own good. If anything, I was the one who blundered. Mrs Peterson warned me that I was overdoing things when you broke down during your run together. I'm afraid I didn't listen. If anything, I think I emboldened you to continue with your investigations."

Judy turned her head away and opened her eyes. "How long did you know?"

"What, that Miss Miller was actually Molenaar, just as my family name is Pietersen, not Peterson? I realised she was Boer years ago. It was something about the way she spoke."

"She sounded English."

"One can lose one's accent, particularly in childhood, but intonation and speech patterns tend to stay. In any case, it is always hardest to hide one's background from another person of the same lineage." Peterson gave up waiting for Judy to turn and face him, and turned towards the window. He could see an ambulance parked to the side of the front door and a couple of patients enjoying the afternoon sunshine. It could not be long, he thought, before all hell broke loose and the place was overrun with injured and dying soldiers. The London hospitals were already full and struggling. The steady creep of casualties would continue across the country until every hospital bed was accounted for. "I knew what Miss Miller was up to shortly before the beginning of term. She made a mistake, an oversight. We worked it out only very shortly before you began to suspect."

"I do wish you'd trusted me," said Judy quietly. "I thought you all had it in for me."

"I owe you an apology for that," said Peterson awkwardly. "You've had a hellish term, mostly through no fault of your own, but it was for your own safety. The sad thing is that Miss Miller was a lousy spy—she left clues all over the place but no evidence, and one cannot accuse a person without evidence. But that didn't mean she wasn't dangerous. In real life, when a spy is uncovered, he can do only one of two things—kill the witness or kill himself. If she hadn't been so desperate to retrieve the letter you stole, she might well have silenced you and fled."

"So I killed her instead."

Peterson was at Judy's side again in an instant. "Judy, turn around and look at me," he instructed her. "Look me in the eye. Come on." Judy turned onto her back with the utmost reluctance, flinching as the mattress began to press against bruises she had not noticed before. "You must understand this, or it will haunt you all your life: the only person at

189

fault here was Miss Miller. Certainly, she had suffered very greatly, but many of us suffered and did not make the decisions she made. She took her own life."

Judy stared up at the ceiling, examining the many hairline cracks in the whitewash. "I had no idea Annie was involved," said Judy lamely. "We haven't seen so much of one another this term. I'm afraid I never guessed."

"You aren't the only one. I should have noticed her absences, but if she wasn't at the cottage, I always assumed she was at school. It was easy for her to slip between two stools." He did not add his own guilty reflection, that she was an easy personality to overlook, the sort of girl nobody ever noticed, who would have responded so quickly to anyone who made her feel important and out of the ordinary, or at least made her believe that she had an important mission in life that only she could fulfil. "Please try not to hold it against her," Peterson added. "She's a good girl but not a clever girl, and she's never had to be strong before. I'm sorry to say that she is easily led."

"I should have let her come first," said Judy in a half whisper, plunging the room into silence; no response was necessary. Judy hardly dared to ask the question. "Sir, what is going to happen to the school?"

Peterson shook his head. "It's all right; it is not long until the end of term. The decision has been made to close the school early and send all the girls home. We will reopen in the autumn as always."

"I can't go home. My father will never accept me."

"I had thought of that. I was talking with Mrs Peterson about it before I came to see you, and, well, we both think you should stay with us at the cottage for now."

Judy's eyes widened. "Is that allowed?"

"Of course it is. You could always teach at the school until your eighteenth birthday. Then you could choose your own work without the need for parental permission." Judy's eyes were glazing over again. "Look here, don't think about it now; it's a lot for you to take in. Save your energies for making a good recovery. The future can wait."

"The future won't happen," said Judy coldly. "Mine won't, anyhow; she said so." Tears were coming again, and she was too exhausted to fight them. "She said they'd hang me. When they come. And they will come."

Judy felt the weight of a hand pressing gently against her head, but she could not stop crying. It was such a very long time since she had felt close to anyone that the gesture of affection was more than she could cope with, and she lost herself in the whirlpool of conflicting emotions, knowing that there was someone waiting to pull her to safety if she were dragged down.

"Judy, you mustn't be afraid," said a calm, authoritative voice above the storm. "I should have told you this a long time ago. Please don't be frightened. You are perfectly safe with us."

"They'll come for me. I saw the stories in the newspaper. They won't care that I go to Mass on Sunday; I'm a Jew."

"Judy, open your eyes." The effect was pointless; even with her eyes open, she was so blinded by tears, she could hardly see.

Judy covered her eyes with the corner of her bedsheet, as much to avoid having to look at him as anything else. "Thank you," she managed to say, though it hardly sounded adequate.

"Who knows," Peterson continued more cheerfully, "it might not happen at all. We're not beaten yet. Please God, we won't be."

~

It was nearly a week later that Mr Forbes came to the hospital to drive Judy back to the school. She had been visited every day by one or other member of the Peterson clan, but she had not set eyes on Mr Forbes since he had dragged her away from Elsa Miller's presence. Forbes' manner was awkwardly jovial as he helped her into the car. "I've come to spring you from jail!" he declared dramatically. "I'm amazed you didn't make a break for it yourself!"

The ice broke between them as soon as it became apparent that Harry Forbes was an appallingly bad driver. "Mr Peterson filled in all the missing details," said Judy quickly as they thundered down the road. "I'm sorry about it all. I'm sorry about your head. Or was it your neck? There, I've said it now."

"It's all right, Judy," Forbes promised. "You're good at working out puzzles, I must say. But I've always known that."

"I'm not sure I know what to do when I've solved them, though," Judy responded. "But thanks anyway, sir."

Forbes was silent a long time before speaking again. "You know, Judy, I think you should stop calling me 'sir'. You're not my pupil anymore, and I'm not a teacher."

Judy looked at him in alarm. "What's happened? Mr Peterson said the school would open again in the autumn."

"Yes, and it will," Forbes promised, "but I'm afraid I won't be there."

"Is it because of me? Is it because of what happened?"

"No, no, not at all. Please don't think this has anything to do with it. I've been—well, I suppose you could say I've been called up."

"But you can't be a soldier, sir!" She remembered herself. "Sorry, but you can't."

"I'm not going to fight, Judy—not like that, anyway." Forbes slowed the car down as he turned onto the avenue lined with overarching beech trees. Judy began to fidget. "It will feel a little strange to begin with, being back here with all the girls gone, but you know, it's only what it's like for Annie Peterson and the others who live here."

"I'm not sure I can bear to go anywhere near the sports pavilion again," confessed Judy, "or the headmistress' study."

"It will take time, but you'll recover," promised Forbes, manoeuvring the car clumsily round a bend in the road. He came to a halt and parked the car. "You're strong. Mr Peterson said you never gave away a word, even when she did that"—he pointed at Judy's plaster cast, which Annie had vandalised with her signature and a scattering of badly drawn stars. Yellow, six-pointed stars.

"Why have we stopped? Is something wrong?"

"I thought you might like a little walk first. You've been cooped up in bed all week."

Judy tried desperately to hide her excitement as he helped her out of the car and led her through the line of trees into a forbidden area of scrubland behind. It was forbidden territory only because there was a small ornamental lake that a group of third formers had been caught paddling in once, but it was almost an act of initiation to be escorted there. The childhood rules no longer applied. "Last time I set foot in here, I got a frightful pasting," said Judy, provoking laughter from Forbes. "It was in my first term. I didn't realise it was out of bounds until Miss Gibbs was fishing me out."

"It's all going to change now, Judy," said Forbes, turning to face her. He realised she must have only rarely been alone in male company, and she blushed as soon as they made eye contact. She already looked older than just over a week before, but that could only be expected of a person who had witnessed death—and an unnatural death at that. Judy's more mature look was helped by the fact that a nurse had evidently insisted upon combing her hair, and it was pinned back at one side quite elegantly. Mrs Peterson had taken Judy a clean blouse, skirt and green cardigan to wear, but she must have given up on finding a pair of stockings without holes in them, and stockings were already hard to come by. The crocheted white socks rather spoilt the adult style into which Judy was being initiated.

"I'm not sure I'm ready yet," admitted Judy. "A week ago, I was still sitting on a school bench."

"It will feel strange to begin with."

"Strange?" exclaimed Judy. "I shall feel frightened to go into the staff room in case someone raps me over the knuckles!" She hesitated. "I do wish you weren't going. You're quite young; I shouldn't feel so out of place."

Forbes suppressed a groan. He was twenty-two years old, but in the eyes of a girl just six years younger than he, he was already getting on a bit. "Stay close to the Petersons; they'll look after you. I can't think of better mentors for you than those two, and they've been teachers for many years." He took a risk and reached out to take her hand. "Let's walk a little farther, shall we?"

Judy let him take her hand and lead her to the edge of the

water. It was odd, but she was sure she remembered the lake being much larger and more dramatic than it looked now. It was hardly more than a large ditch filled with brackish water; a lonely heron looked up at them suspiciously before continuing to look for food. "The Petersons have always been so kind to me," she said. "They're the only real family I've had since my mother died. I just can't bear the idea of staying here after what's happened."

Forbes felt her squeezing his hand encouragingly. He knew he could say it. "I don't want you to stay here, Judy. I want to take you with me." He had said it wrong; she pulled her hand away, more in surprise than indignation. She was too curious to be offended. "Not like that, I mean. What I mean is . . ." He looked up at the dappled sky for inspiration, but none came. He said it anyway. "I mean that I want you to join me in my work. There are other positions opening up for mathematicians and I think it might suit you."

"But I'm not allowed to do anything unless my father says so," protested Judy, "and you haven't even said what you're doing!"

"You won't need his permission to do this. In fact, I doubt you will be allowed to discuss it with him," explained Harry. "Look, I wasn't lying when I told you I was preparing you for the Oxford entrance exam. I meant you to take it, and I am sorry that that will not be possible now. But I had other plans as well."

"The special exam I was going to sit at school? All that maths you made me do and you wouldn't tell me why?"

"You have to understand, Judy, I am new here. I didn't know any of you well and I needed to know just how good a mathematician you are. And you are one of the best."

Judy felt her face overheating and turned away, sitting herself down at the side of the lake. "Thank you, sir."

"Do you suppose you could get used to calling me Harry?" Forbes asked. "It would make life a little easier between us."

"I rather think not, but I can always try, I suppose." She made an elaborate display of loosening and tying her shoes. "I'm afraid I still do not quite understand what you are talking about, sir. Harry." She giggled. "I say, that does sound funny."

"Judy, you are not just a mathematician, you are good at working out puzzles. There is a need for people who are good with figures, good at noticing patterns and codes. It would be the perfect work for you. Frankly, I can't see you coping with the discipline of nursing or the tedium of working in a factory."

Forbes sat down next to Judy and took out a small paper bag from his pocket. "How long do I have to think about it?" she asked, reaching into the bag. It was full of mint humbugs. "Thank you, Harry."

They sat together watching the insects buzzing across the surface of the water. Judy felt mosquitoes prickling her bare knees but could not bring herself to move. For years to come, the sticky taste of peppermint would always remind her of the first confused stirrings of attraction she had ever felt, but for the moment, they were two young people enjoying a peaceful summer afternoon together, untroubled by a war that had so recently invaded their lives.

13

"You must be desperate for that thing to come off," said Annie, pointing at Judy's plaster cast. "It must be terribly annoying."

"Only in that it feels like having a rolling pin instead of an arm," commented Judy. "It's funny the way one gets used to things."

In all honesty, Annie was probably more desperate for Judy's plaster cast to come off then Judy was; it had fairly terrible associations for both of them. Unfortunately, Annie's mother had told Annie that Judy would be in plaster for weeks, since wrists were a nuisance to mend at the best of times and it had been so badly broken. Annie had regretted bringing up the conversation then and rather regretted it now, but part of her was trying desperately to talk about what had happened without mentioning anything important. There were so many mundane reasons to have a plaster cast; girls got them falling off ponies and out of trees. There was a comforting innocence to the sight of it.

"As long as I can still run, I don't mind," promised Judy. "The headmistress was kind enough to break my left wrist anyway, so that it wouldn't interfere with my schoolwork." She giggled, but for once it was Annie who couldn't see the joke. "Not that I expect she imagined I'd be doing this sort of work. I was supposed to be plonked on a train and sent home to my father."

Judy's face clouded over, and they walked through the village in silence. They had been on a stroll to the post office to see if Judy had received a telegram. The journey was unnecessary of course, but Judy kept saying that she wouldn't want to waste the time of the telegram boy if she could pick up the message herself, and the Petersons knew that she was so desperate to receive a message of some kind from her father that there was little point in telling her not to bother looking. Both girls suspected that these little trips were being indulged by their elders because it got them out of the house and they both needed to lose their fear of venturing any distance from the cottage again.

For a Londoner, the village held few attractions. There was a post office, a public house from which both girls would have been unceremoniously ejected if they had attempted to enter, a greengrocer, a butcher and a small bakery. Down a few side streets, a short distance from the tiny high street, there was a forge and a tailor's shop, where the proprietress, an elderly Irish woman, was always to be seen sitting outside the shop front on a fine day, chatting to passersby as she went about her handiwork. With the front door permanently ajar, the mechanical murmur of her husband's Singer sewing machine was always to be heard. Rumour had it that Mrs Kelly had been carried to England in a suitcase as a baby when her parents had fled some rebellion or other, but Annie couldn't remember the name of it now. Mrs Kelly waved at the girls as they passed, watching as though she expected them to stop—Annie quite often came to the shop, not to have her clothes mended but to buy one of Mrs Kelly's prize jars of jam. Annie's friendly smile did not waver as they passed, but she could not bring herself to stop in case it started a conversation, and she was still too afraid to talk to anyone outside the family.

The problem with a village was that everyone knew everything. The more Annie thought about it, the more she wondered how on earth she had managed to keep any secret to herself without some nosy parker noticing something, all that curtain twitching, all that gossip floating about. "It must be quite exciting for you to be able to come into the village now, whenever you like," suggested Annie, as they passed the Anglican church. The Church of All Saints was a crumbling, lichen-covered mediaeval pile that had been vandalised and pillaged during the Reformation, its treasures destroyed, the stained-glass windows smashed and every fresco white-washed over, only for the Tractarians to make such things popular again during the previous century, causing an ambitious cleric to put new stained glass in place. He probably did quite a lot else to the interior, but neither Judy nor Annie had ever set foot inside.

"I suppose it's amusing enough to be able to walk off school grounds without getting clobbered," remarked Judy, "but there's not a lot to see, is there? If we walked this far in London, we would have met dozens of people by now, passed goodness knows how many shops. I might even have dragged you onto an omnibus and taken you to the pictures. Not that I suppose I ever will now."

Annie linked arms with Judy. "Don't be sad; he might write to you tomorrow. Maybe he's writing you a very long letter, and you'll find it on the doormat in the morning."

Judy shrugged. "I don't suppose it would make much difference anyway; he wanted me out of London. I suppose I should just like to know he doesn't hate me."

Annie dragged her feet as she walked next to her friend. They were heading in the direction of the woods, and Annie could feel her heart sinking at the sight of the approaching trees. She did not even feel afraid, just irredeemably miserable. "Dad brought me here the other day," she said. "He said it's best to go back to places where there are bad memories, if one can. It's a bit like falling off a bicycle and getting back on again. If one refuses to return, the fear never goes away."

The sight of the trees sprawling into view had felt welcoming once, but Annie could not remember why. She struggled to pick up the thread of the conversation. "Dad always said —well, I think he said he wished he could have gone back to the place where his mother had died, because perhaps it wouldn't feel so terrible now and he wouldn't feel afraid of it. But of course, it was different for him—they sent him to England, and he could never go back."

"I wonder whether it would have been better for her if she could have done the same," suggested Judy. She was referring to Miss Miller, but she still could not bring herself to say the woman's name. "If she'd made peace perhaps, she mightn't have been so angry about everything."

"My father has had this conversation with you too, hasn't he?" said Annie, looking sidelong at Judy. "That's just what he said to me when he brought me here." They walked into the middle of a clearing of trees and looked up at the chestnut tree with its old, abandoned bird box. "Strange to think

I never even knew whom the messages were for, but then I suppose the postman does not know everyone to whom he delivers letters." Not good enough, she cursed herself inwardly; that sounded so like an excuse. The postman was not to blame for anything he delivered; she knew she had been more than a go-between. Annie shook her head to clear her thoughts. "Well?" prompted Annie. "He has talked to you, hasn't he?"

"Of course. He said those things when he took me to the sports pavilion."

"Oh, that's why you came home in such a tizz. I did wonder."

Judy had been unable to speak to anyone about that visit to the sports pavilion. Mr Peterson had insisted that they go. It was no good hiding away, he had told her; she was going to be a teacher at the school now. She would be teaching maths and games to the younger girls, and she would have to go to the sports pavilion many times. "You see, Judy," he had promised, in that ever-reassuring voice of his, "we'll go together and get it over with. Once you've been back once, it won't hurt anymore."

So he had led her by the hand into the pavilion, and she had stood exactly where she remembered the confrontation taking place. She looked around at the javelins and the lacrosse sticks and the cricket bats and the coiled ropes and the wooden benches they used for gym, but almost immediately, she started shaking and felt the tightening around her throat. "Breathe slowly," he said firmly. "Remember, there's nothing bad here. Nothing is going to hurt you; it's just the sports pavilion. You've been here a thousand times. It's little more than a storeroom. Remember, that's all it is."

But Judy could not get the image out of her mind of that dead, skeletal hand or the sound of Miss Miller's warning, which seemed to come to life in that room. That was why she could not breathe—she could feel the rope coiling itself around her neck, the knot tightening behind her left ear. In the end, Mr Peterson had had to lead her outside so that she could get some fresh air.

"Jude, we ought to get home," said Annie, intruding upon Judy's thoughts. "I told Mother we'd be home in time for tea."

"I shall feel better when I'm teaching," declared Judy, as they took the path to the school at a brisk walk. "I shall feel as though I'm giving something back. Your family have been so good to me, but I really rather feel as though I'm borrowing them."

Annie laughed heartily. "You're welcome to borrow my parents anytime you need them," she chuckled. "You've been borrowing them for years; I don't see why you should be worried about it now. I think they'd be offended if you found yourself another family."

"Thanks."

"You mightn't be the only one," said Annie. "Hortense Allan from the fourth form can't go back home to Jersey, now that the Germans are in charge. She is staying with her aunt in Richmond, but she wrote to my mother the other day saying she's hating it. If she doesn't find anywhere else to go for Christmas, she'll probably spend it with us."

The path to the school was over a mile long, meandering beneath trees and between flower beds. It was one of those deceptive winding roads where every turn promised an end to the journey, only to reveal another stretch of path to be walked. Annie watched her friend trotting beside her. On account of Annie's rather longer legs, she was used to watching Judy having to make a little extra effort to keep up with her when they were walking, making small trotting movements in place of Annie's slow, easy strides. Judy had abandoned the hairpins and hat, even though Annie's mother had taken the trouble to remove the band from Judy's school hat to make it look more grown-up, and she was back to her usual tousled self, which Annie rather preferred. As though reading her mind, Judy said, "You don't mind, do you?"

"Mind what?"

"Everything, I suppose. Living with you, not being a pupil anymore. You know, the other things."

Annie laughed. "It's all right, Jude. I used to wish all the time that you could live with us instead of have to go back to the dormitory at the end of the day, and now you can. As a matter of fact, Mr Forbes said I can call him Harry, now that he is not a teacher anymore and he's going away so soon. I know it's different for you—I mean, different with him . . ." She trailed off, unable to keep up the good humour. She didn't mind at all that Judy was being granted entry into the hallowed inner sanctum of the staff room—there had been a time when she had not cared at all that Judy always came first in every race they ever ran, in every test in which they had both participated; but like most girls, she minded just a little that her friend had been noticed by the male of the species before she had. She swallowed hard, remembering herself. "I shan't mind anything, as long as you don't make me call you Miss Randall!" she joked.

"Race you to the courtyard?"

"Rather!"

The two girls ran, forgetting everything in the exhilaration of running as fast as they could down that familiar track to a place they could both call home. A small part of Annie would always be jealous, just a little envious of the friend who was already pulling forward away from her, leaving her to chase her down the twists and turns of the journey home; but there would come a time when she would understand that she had won the greater prize, even if through no effort of her own. Through whatever twist of providence it was that had made their lives so different, Annie had won: Judy's father had turned against her for seeking the truth too zealously, and Annie's father had forgiven her completely, unconditionally, for being drawn into the darkest of lies.

But for now, Annie ran. She ran until she no longer had the breath to call out to her friend to slow down for her.

14

For a blissful month, Judy was granted a carefree youth—
or at least, the closest to one that a member of her generation would ever have. The invasion failed to materialise,
and in the oasis of the now-empty school, Judy, Annie and
Harry could pretend that the war was not happening at all.
They occupied themselves with the production and storage
of food for the winter, rising at dawn to go mushrooming,
tending the vegetable gardens, gathering up the morning's
eggs. Harry taught them the art of pickling and preserving
every spare scrap until the Petersons' cellar was filled to
overflowing with sealed Kilner jars.

"I don't especially like the taste of vinegar," commented
Judy as they set out on one of their many foraging expedi-
tions. Harry had lined the inside of his knapsack with brown
paper to protect it from what he hoped would be a good
harvest, and he carried an old walking stick in one hand,
carefully ensuring that it never touched the ground in case
anyone thought he needed it for support. It would be handy
for pulling down the higher branches to reach those fat clus-
ters of blackberries that got the most sun and were hardest
to pick.

"You'd better get used to it," replied Harry, taking Judy's
hand, "unless you'd rather go hungry."

"I'm not sure I'd given much thought to where food

comes from before we started gathering it ourselves. You know, I can hardly remember what a banana tastes like."

"Don't worry, they're the most overrated fruit in the world," said Harry breezily. "Who needs to go all the way to the tropics when there are apples and pears and blackberries here?"

"Mrs Peterson asked if we might look for some rosehips on our way back," Judy remembered. "She wants to make syrup."

Harry laughed. "She'll be feeding it to you by the spoonful to help you grow."

"It's probably a bit late for that, I'm afraid, but I don't care what she feeds me as long as there is no cod-liver oil. That's one good thing about growing up." Judy risked moving a little closer to Harry so that she could rest her head on his arm, walking in such a way that she could easily make some space between them if necessary, but he put his arm around her shoulder to indicate that he wanted her to stay where she was. She could see the long high brambles coming into view, the vast thorny branches stretching high over their heads and so far along that she could not see an end. "I used to think Eve picked a banana in the garden," Judy mused. "Paradise was far too much to lose for a common or garden apple."

"You know, you really are barking mad," said Harry, giving Judy a squeeze that made her squeak endearingly, "but old man Chesterton would have said that all mathematicians are a bit touched. It comes from trying to cram the universe into our heads."

They had reached the blackberry bushes, and Harry removed his knapsack, pulling it open and setting it down between them. "I do wish this plaster cast could come off," Judy complained, carefully picking the berries off their spiky branches. "I've got quite used to doing everything one-handed, but still."

"It'll be off before you know it," promised Harry. "Remember, don't pick the fruit too low down. Imagine the height of a dog or a fox."

There was something incredibly satisfying about the touch of the plump fruit between eager fingers and the sight of the cavernous knapsack slowly filling up. Judy concentrated on the branches within easy reach, whilst Harry stood next to her, reaching up above her head to bag the higher ones. There was no practical reason for the two of them to stand quite so close together, since the bramble hedges were so extensive; but they were at that early stage of courtship, in which there were never enough excuses to entwine themselves around one another. "I wish you didn't have to go," said Judy, then immediately wondered whether she had spoilt the moment. "I mean, I wish you could still be a teacher."

Harry looked down at Judy's solemn face. They were standing in a pose that should have been achingly romantic: a handsome young man glancing down at his beloved in a peaceful corner of the English countryside, the bees buzzing lazily in the distance, the sun wrapping their bodies in light —except that Judy had been unable to resist the temptation to snack on some of the blackberries she had been picking and had sticky traces of the evidence around her mouth. The effect was so ludicrous that Harry began laughing uncontrollably, throwing his arms around her waist and lifting her off her feet when he had intended to kiss her.

And Judy laughed, in spite of her sense of mortification

that she had fouled up the situation again. Harry pulled her away from the brambles, spinning her round and round as she laughed, until they were both out of breath and tumbled onto the grass. "I'll call for you," he whispered, tracing his fingers through her inviting black curls. "I promise you, as soon as there is a place for you, I'll send for you—though, of course, you might enjoy teaching so much that you won't want to come. Miss Randall."

The thought that she was soon to be entrusted with the education of young children set Judy's giggles off again, and she was still laughing as Harry leaned forward to kiss her. They were so engrossed with one another that neither of them noticed Annie watching them from the distance, unwilling to interrupt the moment. She had thought better of staying at home that morning and gone out to join them, only to find the two of them curled up together in the grass, too close to each other and far too affectionate for her to write them off as mere friends. Annie watched in silence at the opening up of a world into which she knew she was not welcome, comforting herself that Harry would soon be gone and she could have her old friend back, as though it could possibly be that simple for Judy to slip from the role of sweetheart to a girl's best friend. When Harry finally heaved himself to his feet and helped Judy up so that they could continue with their harvest, Annie counted to twenty before scurrying up to them so that they would think she had just appeared.

Minutes later, the three of them were chatting away, their bare arms covered in scratches, their fingers busy gathering for the winter. And Annie told herself she did not mind. It was better to be Annie Peterson with a home and a family and nothing to worry about anymore than to be a brilliant girl without a home and with a daddy who wouldn't talk to her. How would she have liked to have been abducted at gunpoint and had her wrist broken and had to be rescued? Annie suppressed the repeated thought that she would have rather gone through something like that if it had meant not being the one who committed the crime of being too easy to deceive and threaten.

"Why don't you girls carry on here for a while longer? I'm going in search of rose hips", suggested Harry, doing Annie the favour of breaking into her thoughts. "There are plenty of blackberries to be getting on with at the moment. We might even need to take some home in a while."

Annie wondered sheepishly whether Harry had read her mind and was leaving the two of them to chat privately in his absence. "Judy, I'm so glad you're here," Annie forced herself to say only to discover she meant it. "I'm so glad you didn't have to go. Home wouldn't feel the same without you now."

Judy smiled with the happiness of a person who is used to being in the way or out of place, but part of her was relieved Harry had forbidden her to speak of his plans. The thought of leaving her old friend behind when a new life called felt like a betrayal, even if the cottage would still be a home to return to on leave, but it did not enter Judy's mind that Annie too might be called away one day to do her duty in some far-flung part of the country. On that late August day, Annie Peterson was still the girl who came second, and Judy was still incapable of holding back to let her slip past her across the finishing line.

On another sunny afternoon, as the days of August trickled away, Judy helped Harry to construct a large rabbit hutch, big enough to house as many as twenty rabbits. Judy was not of a practical disposition, but she obediently passed him nails and helped Harry to unroll lengths of chicken wire whilst he drove stakes into the ground and chiselled and hammered until exhaustion overcame him and Judy ran to the house for water. The date of Harry's departure was creeping ever nearer, and he was working more energetically, keen to leave the Petersons with everything they could possibly need before he went away.

When Mrs Peterson came home with the two breeding rabbits she had managed to purchase from a local farmer, Judy fell in love with the biscuit-brown fur balls and named them Winston and Clemmie. She was so blissfully unaware that the rabbits were being bred for food that she treated them as her own beloved pets, holding them in her arms for hours at a time and feeding them dandelion leaves. When she went back to the Petersons' for Christmas at the end of that year, Mr Peterson was forced to fib that Clemmie had done a runner, rather than break it to Judy that little Clemmie was sizzling in small pieces in the pot Judy was stirring, while the rest of her had been turned into a rather fetching muff for Annie's Christmas present. It was amazing what a keen mind could fail to work out, and it saved him the embarrassment of having to admit that he had wept after bashing Clemmie over the head and had to leave his wife to skin her.

When Judy looked back on that short, breathtaking journey to adulthood, she remembered the long hours of daylight and the liberation of being allowed to go running as far as she wanted without worrying about bells and timetables and the prospect of getting into trouble. She wallowed in the memory of picnics under shady trees with Annie increasingly taking on the role of chaperone, surrounded by the aroma of freshly cut grass and the lilac water Harry had bought her.

She chose to forget her many futile visits to the post office to see if her father had answered her letter desperately trying to mend fences. She did not dwell on the terrible afternoon when she was helping Mrs Peterson in the kitchen and they started making mock marzipan with mashed potato and a few drops of almond essence. It took only a few drops for Judy to start smelling cyanide everywhere, a moment before her knees gave way. She did not need to remember how death had haunted her that summer and never really left her alone again.

At the end of August, Harry Forbes packed his trunk and made his way to an unknown destination, leaving Judy with a post office address to write to and a promise—much repeated—that he would send for her as soon as a place became available for her. Another flashpoint in memory: standing tearfully on the railway platform with Harry leaning out of the train window, making a solemn good-bye. It was almost like stepping into a film, thought Judy, as she ran alongside the disappearing train, stopping only when she ran out of platform and was forced to watch the last carriages disappearing along the track in a cloud of steam. It was so very like being the heroine of a tragic cinematic offering, except that a real heroine would have been a few inches taller, would have remembered her hat and gloves and would have stood in poignant silence on the platform, dabbing her streaming eyes with a lace handkerchief rather than running like a bat out of hell to race the departing train. And in a real tragedy, Harry would be going off to the front to do something desperately courageous, fatal and futile, when Judy knew he would be safely home for Christmas if she did not meet him at his secret place of work first.

Nevertheless, it was a subdued Judy who joined the family for dinner that night and who insisted upon going out running a little earlier and for rather longer than was strictly necessary, every day for the last weeks before the school opened again and girls returned from all over the country to begin the new academic year.

~

There was everything and nothing left to say about Judy and that quiet little corner of England where she learnt all the great lessons of life: what it meant to be hated and what it meant to be loved—most of all to be loved. The summer ended without the appearance of German invaders but with the terror and destruction of the Blitz over faraway London. Mr Peterson had fallen into the habit of trying to hide the news from his family, but Judy insisted upon listening to every news bulletin, albeit carefully filtered by the BBC home service. In her determination to keep abreast of all the latest developments, she would rush directly to the wireless in the staff room at morning break, lunchtime and tea break, prompting Mr Peterson to remove it, claiming that it was broken.

The deceit was unnecessary in the end. When the telegram boy appeared at the cottage gate on his bicycle and handed Mary Peterson a message for Judy from her father's solicitor, Judy stopped seeking out news of what was happening to London, as it no longer felt relevant. She greeted the news of her father's death with stony silence and spent the one week's leave Mr Peterson insisted she take, running deep into the countryside for hours at a time or sitting in her room puzzling over ever more complex mathematical equations. She was not to return to London until after VE Day, and by then, her father's executors had sold the surviving house and its contents, leaving her with a generous inheritance and no other evidence that her life with her parents had ever happened.

Perhaps it was best that way, that brutal scrubbing of the past in a world where so much was being obliterated and rewritten. It fitted somehow with the strange hinterland in which Judy found herself when Harry, true to his word, sent for her in November of that year, just halfway through the autumn term. She had never been a personality intended for the classroom and suspected that Mr Peterson felt a little relief when she handed in her notice, though he was too kind and felt too great an affection for her to appear anything other than saddened by the news that she had been called up to use her mathematical skills in the service of king and country.

Of Judy's destination, all that she could say was that it was a magnet for mathematical minds who were good at finding patterns and breaking codes, where the eccentricities and social shortcomings of the many colourful individuals there were quietly tolerated. The work was so secret that Judy and Harry could never speak of it to anyone, even after many years of marriage, and the generation who served there were almost all dead by the time anything could be written about it.

Judy could at least comfort herself that she had done her duty to her country and the cause of freedom, albeit from the safety of a desk, and that it was likely that her work had saved many lives, even if she could never know for certain. And the long years of intense intellectual activity dragged her mind away from that summer night in the sports pavilion, with its cold, unfulfilled prophecies and the sight of a death Judy would always believe she had caused.

In early December 1940, as Judy was settling into her new life, she received a letter from Mr Peterson informing her that Miss Miller's official cause of death was to be a sudden, unexpected heart attack. The true cause of death was not being concealed for Judy's benefit, but she took some comfort from it nonetheless. In later years, as memories began to blur and few were left to remember that night, the official version of events came to feel so much more plausible to Judy than her tormented memories of a stolen letter, abduction and suicide. Indeed, it was hard to remember which memory was true and which was false.